THE EARL ELOPES

Yet finally the Earl's feet were free and he then stood up holding his arms above his head.

Melva had been watching him and she had prayed all the time she had worked on the rope round his hands.

Now she gave a cry of delight,

"We are free! We are free!"

Without thinking she flung herself against the Earl.

He brought down his arms from above his head and put them round her.

Just for a moment he hugged her.

Then without even meaning to his lips found hers.

He kissed her and they were both very still.

With an effort the Earl said,

"Come, let's get out of here."

His voice sounded strange even to himself.

Without glancing at Melva, he walked through the opening into the larger cavern.

He hurried towards the far end of it and she had to run to keep up with him.

By the time she caught up with him he was already walking back over the slippery rocks.

She had led him before, but now he was leading her.

THE BARBARA CARTLAND PINK COLLECTION

Titles in this series

1. The Cross Of Love
2. Love In The Highlands
3. Love Finds The Way
4. The Castle Of Love
5. Love Is Triumphant
6. Stars In The Sky
7. The Ship Of Love
8. A Dangerous Disguise
9. Love Became Theirs
10. Love Drives In
11. Sailing To Love
12. The Star Of Love
13. Music Is The Soul Of Love
14. Love In The East
15. Theirs To Eternity
16. A Paradise On Earth
17. Love Wins In Berlin
18. In Search Of Love
19. Love Rescues Rosanna
20. A Heart In Heaven
21. The House Of Happiness
22. Royalty Defeated By Love
23. The White Witch
24. They Sought Love
25. Love Is The Reason For Living
26. They Found Their Way To Heaven
27. Learning To Love
28. Journey To Happiness
29. A Kiss In The Desert
30. The Heart Of Love
31. The Richness Of Love
32. For Ever And Ever
33. An Unexpected Love
34. Saved By An Angel
35. Touching The Stars
36. Seeking Love
37. Journey To Love
38. The Importance Of Love
39. Love By The Lake
40. A Dream Come True
41. The King Without A Heart
42. The Waters Of Love
43. Danger To The Duke
44. A Perfect Way To Heaven
45. Follow Your Heart
46. In Hiding
47. Rivals For Love
48. A Kiss From The Heart
49. Lovers In London
50. This Way To Heaven
51. A Princess Prays
52. Mine For Ever
53. The Earl's Revenge
54. Love At The Tower
55. Ruled By Love
56. Love Came From Heaven
57. Love And Apollo
58. The Keys Of Love
59. A Castle Of Dreams
60. A Battle Of Brains
61. A Change Of Hearts
62. It Is Love
63. The Triumph Of Love
64. Wanted – A Royal Wife
65. A Kiss Of Love
66. To Heaven With Love
67. Pray For Love
68. The Marquis Is Trapped
69. Hide And Seek For Love
70. Hiding From Love
71. A Teacher Of Love
72. Money Or Love
73. The Revelation Is Love
74. The Tree Of Love
75. The Magnificent Marquis
76. The Castle
77. The Gates Of Paradise
78. A Lucky Star
79. A Heaven On Earth
80. The Healing Hand
81. A Virgin Bride
82. The Trail To Love
83. A Royal Love Match
84. A Steeplechase For Love
85. Love At Last
86. Search For A Wife
87. Secret Love
88. A Miracle Of Love
89. Love And The Clans
90. A Shooting Star
91. The Winning Post Is Love
92. They Touched Heaven
93. The Mountain Of Love
94. The Queen Wins
95. Love And The Gods
96. Joined By Love
97. The Duke Is Deceived
98. A Prayer For Love
99. Love Conquers War
100. A Rose In Jeopardy
101. A Call Of Love
102. A Flight To Heaven
103. She Wanted Love
104. A Heart Finds Love
105. A Sacrifice For Love
106. Love's Dream In Peril
107. Soft, Sweet And Gentle
108. An Archangel Called Ivan
109. A Prisoner In Paris
110. Danger In The Desert
111. Rescued By Love
112. A Road To Romance
113. A Golden Lie
114. A Heart Of Stone
115. The Earl Elopes

THE EARL ELOPES

BARBARA CARTLAND

Barbaracartland.com Ltd

First published on the internet in April 2014
by Barbaracartland.com Ltd

ISBN 978-1-78213-477-0

Printed and bound in Great Britain
by Mimeo of Huntingdon, Cambridgeshire.

THE BARBARA CARTLAND PINK COLLECTION

Dame Barbara Cartland is still regarded as the most prolific bestselling author in the history of the world.

In her lifetime she was frequently in the Guinness Book of Records for writing more books than any other living author.

Her most amazing literary feat was to double her output from 10 books a year to over 20 books a year when she was 77 to meet the huge demand.

She went on writing continuously at this rate for 20 years and wrote her very last book at the age of 97, thus completing an incredible 400 books between the ages of 77 and 97.

Her publishers finally could not keep up with this phenomenal output, so at her death in 2000 she left behind an amazing 160 unpublished manuscripts, something that no other author has ever achieved.

Barbara's son, Ian McCorquodale, together with his daughter Iona, felt that it was their sacred duty to publish all these titles for Barbara's millions of admirers all over the world who so love her wonderful romances.

So in 2004 they started publishing the 160 brand new Barbara Cartlands as *The Barbara Cartland Pink Collection*, as Barbara's favourite colour was always pink – and yet more pink!

The Barbara Cartland Pink Collection is published monthly exclusively by Barbaracartland.com and the books are numbered in sequence from 1 to 160.

Enjoy receiving a brand new Barbara Cartland book each month by taking out an annual subscription to the Pink Collection, or purchase the books individually.

The Pink Collection is available from the Barbara Cartland website www.barbaracartland.com via mail order and through all good bookshops.

In addition Ian and Iona are proud to announce that The Barbara Cartland Pink Collection is now available in ebook format as from Valentine's Day 2011.

For more information, please contact us at:

Barbaracartland.com Ltd.
Camfield Place
Hatfield
Hertfordshire AL9 6JE
United Kingdom

Telephone: +44 (0)1707 642629
Fax: +44 (0)1707 663041
Email: info@barbaracartland.com

THE LATE DAME BARBARA CARTLAND

Barbara Cartland who sadly died in May 2000 at the age of nearly 99 was the world's most famous romantic novelist who wrote 723 books in her lifetime with worldwide sales of over 1 billion copies and her books were translated into 36 different languages.

As well as romantic novels, she wrote historical biographies, 6 autobiographies, theatrical plays, books of advice on life, love, vitamins and cookery. She also found time to be a political speaker and television and radio personality.

She wrote her first book at the age of 21 and this was called *Jigsaw*. It became an immediate bestseller and sold 100,000 copies in hardback and was translated into 6 different languages. She wrote continuously throughout her life, writing bestsellers for an astonishing 76 years. Her books have always been immensely popular in the United States, where in 1976 her current books were at numbers 1 & 2 in the B. Dalton bestsellers list, a feat never achieved before or since by any author.

Barbara Cartland became a legend in her own lifetime and will be best remembered for her wonderful romantic novels, so loved by her millions of readers throughout the world.

Her books will always be treasured for their moral message, her pure and innocent heroines, her good looking and dashing heroes and above all her belief that the power of love is more important than anything else in everyone's life.

"True love has been sought by men and women since Adam and Eve and I am often asked, 'how do I know if it really is true love' and I always give the same answer, 'don't ask me, ask your heart'."

Barbara Cartland

CHAPTER ONE
1872

The Earl of Bourne, driving his team of chestnut horses, was thinking with great delight how excellent they were.

He had purchased them at Tattersalls a fortnight earlier.

Their previous owner had died and left a huge pile of debts and thinking of debts made the Earl remember that he had not yet paid for this superb team.

The reason that he was going home was to see his father about his overdraft.

The Duke of Shelbourne had made it very clear the last time that his son, Clive, had come to see him.

His large number of huge bills were something that was not to occur again.

Unfortunately the Earl had by now been enjoying himself in London.

And that was expensive, especially when his wild extravagance included an extremely attractive young girl who was a dancer at *The Drury Lane Theatre*.

As he drove out of London and the traffic was less, the Earl increased the pace of his horses.

He thought that he would like to achieve the record to Shelbourne Towers in Oxfordshire and there was little reason to doubt that he would be successful.

Reflectively he began to rehearse in his mind what he would say to his father.

He knew that conversations about money invariably ended in a flaming row and this, however, did not only just apply to money.

The Duke of Shelbourne was a very rich man and he could therefore well afford his only son's extravagance.

What infuriated him was that the boy had refused to marry.

"We have to have an heir to all this," the Duke had said not once but a thousand times.

"I do realise that, Papa," the Earl invariably replied. "But there is plenty of time and I will be extremely careful not to die without having provided you with a grandson or two."

He meant this to be a joke, but the Duke did not think it funny.

He had suffered agonies when the Earl had been serving abroad with his Regiment.

The moment he returned and decided he wanted to resign his Commission, the Duke had heaved a large sigh of relief.

"Now," he said to his relations, "Clive will settle down and have a family. Heaven knows, there are enough women for him to choose from!"

The Duke appreciated that his son was at the top of the list of London hostesses as a most eligible bachelor.

He was not only the heir to the Dukedom, he was outstandingly handsome, intelligent and good at any game he turned his hand to.

He also, as those who knew him well were aware, had considerable charm.

This with his good-looks made him irresistible to women.

The Duke knew perfectly well that there was important family in the whole of the country who wou welcome his son with open arms and they would be to boast that he had married one of their daughters.

At twenty-eight Clive was still unmarried.

He was wise enough to keep well away fror *debutantes* who were a snare for any bachelor and c avoided invitations from his father's friends with y daughters.

Instead he enjoyed himself with married ladies had complacent husbands.

And he really enjoyed the allure of the wome saw behind the footlights and he met them in the n nightclubs he frequented with his gentlemen friends.

The only difficulty was that such pleasures v extremely expensive and his father resented having to for them.

As the Earl drove on, he was totting up a list of items he was carrying bills for.

The horses he was driving had been very expensi largely because there had been several others older th himself bidding for them.

The diamond bracelet he had given the adoral Fifi had naturally delighted her and there was, however, doubt that his father would consider the cost involved unnecessary frippery and luxury.

'For the pleasure she has given me,' he thoug defiantly, 'I should have given her the necklace to mat it!'

But he knew that he was not brave enough to do s

As it was there were enormous bills for clothes a there was also a big bill for a party he had given for one his friends on his birthday.

It had certainly been a success and they had drunk an abnormal amount of champagne.

And the entertainers whom the Earl had engaged for the night had cost rather more than the wine.

He knew that his father would be very annoyed when he saw the pile of bills.

Undoubtedly once again he would beg him to settle down.

He could take over the running of one of the large estates that had been owned by the Dukes of Shelbourne for generations and there was certainly a wide choice all over the country.

The present Duke quite rightly thought that all this would be an attraction to any man.

Shelbourne Towers had ten thousand acres of land surrounding it.

There was a very pleasant house at Newmarket where the Earl kept his racehorses and there were three thousand well-tended acres attached to that property.

The Duke owned a castle in Scotland with twenty-two thousand acres of moorland, which provided him with the best grouse shooting in the country.

Besides this, there were several rivers that were teeming with salmon.

There was another house, the Earl remembered, in Huntingdonshire that had belonged to his mother's family and she had left it on her death to her grandson 'when he married.'

It was, he knew, just another inducement to push him up the aisle and, because it annoyed him, he had not paid a visit to this house or its surrounding acreage since his grandmother had died.

'The whole thing is ridiculous,' he told himself as his horses increased their speed. 'There is plenty of time

for me to produce a dozen heirs. I will marry when I find someone to live with who will not bore me after the first twenty-four hours.'

He thought it over and then changed the target to twenty-four months.

'If I can survive that length of time, I can survive anything,' he mused.

So far since he had been in London after he had left his Regiment he had not been in the slightest attracted to any young unmarried woman.

He had not even seen one who made him feel it imperative for him to take the trouble to get to know her.

He had spent so much time with those who were on the stage.

He liked women who walked lightly in the way that made it impossible for a man not to notice their charms and the exquisite curves of their figures.

He liked a woman he could laugh with and one who had a quick repartee that was amusing and provocative.

How, he asked himself again, was he going to find anything like that in a young girl who had just left the schoolroom?

She would doubtless have been badly educated by a Governess who knew little more than she knew herself.

Vaguely at the back of his mind he had a plan.

Perhaps in ten years' time he would find a widow who was still young enough to give him the much wanted heir.

She would be experienced in the ways of the world and would keep him amused and content.

This all passed through his mind.

He was driving now through the countryside with the sun shining on the sprouting cornfields and primroses were glinting yellow in the hedgerows.

'Tomorrow,' the Earl thought, 'I will ride over Papa's acres that I know are the envy of the local landlords and see how well we '*plough the fields and scatter*'.'

He always enjoyed one special activity when he went home.

No matter how difficult his father was there were always the horses in the stables.

The Duke prided himself on having a better stable than anyone else and his horses won a great number of the Classic races every year,

The Earl had been able to ride almost before he could walk.

He had naturally joined the Household Brigade because it was a Cavalry Regiment, but he had, however, thought that the horses provided by the Brigade were not good enough for him.

He had usually supplied his own charger and he was teased by his fellow Officers as having more horses than women.

"It's not surprising," the Earl would reply. "I find them more attractive, swifter and easier to control!"

They had all laughed at this, but they envied him.

He remembered now that his last mount, of whom he had been incredibly fond, would be waiting for him at Shelbourne Towers.

He reproached himself that he had not been home for some months and the horse would undoubtedly have missed him.

'If Papa is not too disagreeable about my bills,' he told himself, 'I must stay in the country for a week or so and ride Crusader every day as he would expect me to do.'

The idea cheered him up and it made him not so apprehensive as to what would occur when he arrived at his home.

Driving to Shelbourne Towers usually took about three hours and the Earl stopped on the way for luncheon at the cosy Posting inn he always patronised.

The publican was delighted to see him and greeted him warmly.

By the time he had sat down at the luncheon table, a bottle of his favourite champagne had been put on ice and the chef was preparing the special dishes that they knew he favoured.

"It's bin too long since you visited us, my Lord," the publican said. "But I've seen your name in *The Court Circular* and knows your Lordship's been enjoyin' 'imself in London."

"There are just too many parties," the Earl replied, "and I am looking forward to being back in the country."

"That's just as it should be, my Lord," the publican said, "and I'm sure there'll be a right big welcome for you at The Towers."

The Earl was not certain of this, so he did not reply.

He merely enjoyed every mouthful of the excellent dishes the inn's chef had cooked for him.

It meant, of course, that he must leave a large tip for him with the publican.

When he came out of the inn, he could see that his groom had watered the horses and the rest had made them eager to be on their way again.

He patted each horse before he climbed into the driving seat.

He was thinking, as he did so, that he had never seen a team to rival them.

"Everyone's been admirin' your 'orses, my Lord," the groom said. "Most didn't believe it'd be possible to find four with exactly the same colour and markings."

"I am so lucky to have anything so unique," the Earl replied, "and I hope that His Grace will admire them too."

He thought, as he spoke, that it would be essential for his father to see the horses before he saw the bill.

Then once again, as he drove off, he was wondering what sort of reception he would receive when he finally did arrive.

Shelbourne Towers had been in the Ducal family for five hundred years.

It had been altered considerably from the original design, but fortunately when each generation had added to it, they had still kept some of the oldest features.

With their intricately carved wood panelling and diamond-paned windows the principal rooms were most attractive.

It had been a perfect place for a small boy to play 'hide and seek' and the Earl did so with his friends or with any of the servants who could spare the time.

He had loved all the secret passages that had been added in Cromwell's time.

The Royalists had hidden in them when they were being sought by the Roundheads and the Priests' Hole and the little Chapel were both intact.

What the Earl had enjoyed most was being able to peep into the main rooms without anyone knowing that he was there.

If his father caught him prying on his guests, he would be exceedingly angry, but the Earl had continued to do so.

He learned of *affaires-de-coeur* that no one else was aware of and there were matrimonial rows which he now remembered vividly.

It made him more determined than ever not to get married, unless he was forcibly compelled to do so or if he really fell in love.

He had been totally infatuated, entranced and even bemused by beautiful women.

Yet at the back of his mind he knew that this was not the love that had inspired men since the beginning of civilisation, the love that they had been tortured and even killed for. And to them love was an ideal that they could not ignore.

The Earl drove his team up the long drive with tall lime trees on either side of it.

He reflected that one day it would be all his and it meant a great deal to him. In fact it meant more every time he came home.

The house itself was so beautiful.

With a lake in front of it and dark fir trees behind, it made a glorious picture and many artists over the centuries had tried somewhat ineffectively to portray it on canvas.

The Earl made his horses trot across the bridge over the lake slowly.

He naturally wanted to look for the white swans swimming on the water below him with their baby cygnets trailing behind them.

There were more, he thought, than when he had last visited his home and they certainly made the lake with the kingcups growing round its edges very enchanting.

The Earl drew up outside the front door.

Two footmen in livery ran the red carpet down the steps and he handed his reins to his groom.

"Two hours and three-quarters," he crowed. "If we had not stopped for luncheon, that would undoubtedly be a record."

"'Tis, my Lord. Congratulations!" the groom said. "It be the best drive we 'ave 'ad for a long time."

The Earl smiled and stepped out of the chaise and nodded to the footmen who had laid down the red carpet.

He was greeted by the butler who had been at The Towers ever since he was a small boy.

"It's a pleasure to welcome you back, my Lord," Barker said.

"I am glad to be back," the Earl replied. "Is His Grace in the study?"

"That's where you'll find him, my Lord. His Grace were ever so pleased when he hears you were to arrive this afternoon. It be nigh on three months since we've had the pleasure of your Lordship's company."

The Earl was aware of this, so he did not answer.

He merely walked behind Barker who, he noticed, had rather less hair than on his last visit.

They went down the wide passage that led to the main rooms of the house.

One of these was the study and it was where his father invariably sat when he was alone, writing letters and reading the newspapers.

This was not often, as the Earl was well aware, as there were always members of the family coming to stay, 'for a few nights'.

Two of his more austere maiden aunts had settled in at The Towers for several months.

The Earl was hoping that his father would be alone.

In his last letter he had said that a cousin, who they found a bore, was leaving and had related what a laborious two weeks it had been, but that now she was with her Aunt Margaret.

His father had added at the end of the letter,

"*I hope I shall see you soon.*"

The Earl now felt guilty.

He had come home, not to please his father as he should have done, but because he was in debt.

Barker opened the study door.

"His Lordship, Your Grace," he announced, raising his voice as the Duke was inclined to be deaf.

He was sitting at his writing desk and he looked up as the study door opened.

When he saw his son, he rose to his feet and held out his hand.

"Oh, here you are, Clive," he said. "I began to think that you had forgotten me."

"I have most certainly not done that, Papa," the Earl answered. "But I have so many friends in London that time seems to fly by before one knows what is happening."

"Well, you are here now," the Duke smiled, "and strangely enough I was on the verge of sending for you."

"For any particular reason?" the Earl enquired.

"A very particular one as it so happens," the Duke replied. "But do tell me first why you have come home so unexpectedly."

The Earl drew in his breath.

"I think you can guest the answer, Papa."

The Duke moved towards his son who was standing beside the fireplace.

He was frowning.

"It cannot be possible that you are in debt once again!" he exclaimed.

"I am afraid so, Papa, but I have no wish to upset you."

"Of course it upsets me. I have only just finished paying off your last bills, which appalled me as you well know. I cannot imagine how you could spend so much money in so short a time."

"It's very difficult not to in London. As you well know, Papa, you would not expect me to accept so much hospitality without making any return."

"I agree with that," the Due admitted. "But at the same time I hardly think you need to be overwhelmingly hospitable to a dancer of no particular standing."

That his father knew about Fifi did not surprise the Earl.

Of course, being who he was, he was talked about.

That he gave the gorgeous Fifi supper practically every night after her performance at the theatre was over would be known not only to his contemporaries but to his father's as well.

One of his many relations would be sure to have seen him at *The Drury Lane Theatre* and they would also dine in the restaurants where he entertained Fifi.

He could see all too clearly how they would make quite sure that his father was aware of it and they would write in their letters all too clearly,

"*It has been delightful walking in Rotten Row in the morning. Yesterday morning I saw Clive driving a very smart chaise and with him an extremely striking woman. My escort told me that she appears every night on the stage at The Drury Lane Theatre.*"

If the letter was from one of his younger relatives to whom he had paid little attention, she would make it even more catty.

Aloud the Earl said,

"I know, Papa, that you would not approve. At the same time the lady in question is very attractive and you cannot expect me to behave like a monk in London."

"You certainly don't do that," the Duke responded readily, "and monks, I may point out, dear boy, have no money."

"Which rather applies to me at the moment," the Earl answered a little cheekily.

"You had better tell me the worst before we go any further," the Duke insisted, sitting down in an armchair. "Exactly how much do you owe this time?"

The Earl drew in his breath.

He thought on the whole that it was best to tell the truth and not prevaricate as he often did.

"Nearly twenty thousand pounds, Papa. I am sorry! But that does include the four horses I have driven down with, which I think you will not only admire but admit were a very good buy."

"That is the sort of thing you always say," the Duke retorted. "No buy is a good buy if you cannot afford it. You go too far, Clive, as I have told you before. This time when I pay your bills you will obey me and do what I tell you to do for a change."

"And what is that?" the Earl asked only a little suspiciously.

He was almost certain what the answer would be because he had heard it so often before.

"You will settle down, marry and have an heir," the Duke stipulated. "Actually I was just about to send for you, as I have already chosen your wife with Her Majesty's approval."

The Earl stared at him.

"*You have chosen – my wife*," he said very slowly. "What do you mean by that?"

"Exactly what I say, my boy. You cannot find a wife for yourself, so now I have spoken to Her Majesty the Queen and she agrees with me that it is time you became a serious member of the House of Lords."

"I cannot see," the Earl began, "that the Queen – "

The Duke held up his hand.

"I have not yet finished!" he interrupted him. "Her Majesty has considered your Social importance and that your mother, Princess Louise, was a distant cousin of hers. She has therefore, most graciously, given you permission to marry Princess Gilberta of Saxe-Coburg, who is arriving on a visit to Windsor Castle next week."

For a moment there was complete silence.

Then the Earl blurted out,

"Do you really expect me, Papa, to marry a woman I have never seen and who has been chosen for me by the Queen and I know nothing about her? I would rather jump in the lake and drown myself!"

"Well, that perhaps is what you will do," the Duke replied. "And I have said, on your behalf, that you are extremely honoured at Her Majesty's interest and that you will be delighted to marry the Princess. As is traditional for the Duchess of Shelbourne, she will in time become a Lady of the Bedchamber."

Again there was silence until the Earl quizzed,

"And if I refuse?"

"It would be an insult to Her Majesty and I should feel obliged to express my horror at your disloyalty to the Crown by cutting you out of my will and refusing, in this instance, to pay any of your bills."

"You cannot mean that," the Earl said.

"I do mean it and I mean it most sincerely. You have played about long enough. You are twenty-eight and no longer a beardless boy. Now you will settle down here if you wish or in any of my other houses, you will take your place as you should have done long ago as the future sixth Duke of Shelbourne."

"I refuse! I here and now absolutely refuse to do anything so unnatural and to me utterly repulsive," the Earl countered sharply.

"In which case, as I have already said, it will be an insult to Her Majesty. I can only express my horror at your behaviour and I will cut you off without a penny."

The Earl knew it was impossible for his father to do this.

Yet for the moment all he could think of was that he was going to be saddled with some dull and doubtless plain German woman.

She would, in his mind, speak bad English, while he could not speak a word of German.

He could imagine nothing more ghastly.

He would be tied up in the future in a position from which there was no hope of escape.

With an effort he managed to say,

"Please, Papa, I know that you are angry with me for spending so much money, but *please* don't force me into a marriage that would make me utterly miserable."

"I have given you every chance to find a wife for yourself," the Duke replied. "But you have refused and I have been told on very good authority that you have been boasting that you have no intention of marrying for another twenty years at least."

The Earl knew that this was tittle-tattle from one of his relations.

"I may have said it as a joke," he said quickly, "but I was really waiting to fall in love."

"Which is highly unlikely with the sort of women you spend your time with," his father answered him. "The Countess of Clayton told me that she has asked you four times to dinner parties and you have always refused. The Claytons are as good a family as we are and she has two daughters of the right age."

Trying to remember them, the Earl vaguely had a vision of two rather unappealing young women.

He had avoided them when he had seen them at parties and he had certainly refused the very dull dinners the Countess gave.

She was naturally hoping to catch two important husbands for her dreary daughters.

Aloud he now asked,

"Give me a chance to have another look round, Papa. As I have come down unexpectedly, the Queen will not know you have told me what you planned. You can tell Her Majesty later that, when you did get in touch with me, you found I had already proposed marriage to a very attractive and elegant young woman. Therefore there was nothing I could do about Princess Gilberta."

"I am not listening to you," the Duke said. "When we last talked about your debts, you promised me then you would try to keep within the very generous allowance I give you. I also begged you to get married because it was so vital to the family you should be very proud of."

He paused for a moment and, as his son did not speak, he continued,

"I intend to tell Her Majesty when I go to Windsor Castle the day after tomorrow that you are well aware of how gracious and helpful she has been and that you are looking forward to meeting Princess Gilberta as soon as she arrives in the country."

"I will not do it!" the Earl asserted angrily. "You don't have to live with the woman – I have! I am damned if I will be married to some fat boring German who I doubt knows one end of a horse from the other!"

"I expect that also applies to the dancer with whom you are so enamoured," the Duke replied sarcastically. "It is no use you arguing with me, Clive. I have made up my mind. I shall expect you to obey Her Majesty's command and accept her invitation to meet Princess Gilberta when she arrives at Windsor Castle."

The Duke had risen while he had been speaking.

Now he walked towards the door saying,

"If you don't agree, I do *not* think you will find the alternative particularly attractive which could, of course, eventually mean the Fleet Prison if you don't pay off your debts."

The Duke walked out of the room closing the door sharply behind him.

The Earl put up his hand to his forehead.

He could hardly believe what had just taken place.

His father had faced him with bankruptcy and the only way that he could save himself was by marrying this German woman chosen for him by the Queen.

It was an old joke in the Club that the Queen was marrying off all Prince Albert's relations to distinguished aristocrats from other countries in Europe or England.

So far the English had done rather well in managing to escape her commands.

One Duke, however, had been obliged to accept an extremely plain and unattractive wife and the alternative would have been to give up his distinguished position at Court.

The Earl knew that he was in a trap that it was almost impossible for him to escape from.

Once his father had made up his mind, then nothing would change it.

There was no one the Earl could turn to for help.

He was certain that if his mother had still been alive she would not let this happen.

His father was now surrounded by elderly relatives and they would be delighted to see him taken down a peg or two, simply because they felt that he had been treated as the 'golden boy' for far too long.

'What can I do? What on earth can I do?' the Earl asked himself.

He had never in his wildest dreams thought that he would ever be forced into marriage.

Granted his father had been very disagreeable the last several times he had paid his bills and he had very obviously expected him to obey his instructions.

They were to find a wife before he returned with another bundle of debts.

Marriage to a woman he had never seen, who was a German and with whom he would have no interests at all in common was to him a life sentence.

'If only I had someone to talk to about this,' he said to himself despondently.

Then suddenly he remembered Nanny.

Nanny had been his nurse since he was born and she was now getting on for sixty and over the years she had become one of the family.

She stayed in the nursery upstairs looking after the children of the Bourne relations when they came to stay.

Otherwise, as the Earl knew, she was waiting for him to be married and produce the much-wanted heir to the Dukedom.

If no one else loved him, he knew that Nanny did.

At least she would understand the horror of what faced him at this very moment.

He walked out of the study, across the hall and up the stairs.

He expected that his father had either gone to his own bedroom or he might be out in the garden.

Usually, when the Duke was perturbed or upset by his son or anyone else, he would walk through the woods breathing in the fresh air deeply.

Situated at the back of the house the woods were very quiet and soothing.

The Earl had learned when he was a child that his father usually returned in a better humour and hoped that was what he would be doing now.

He had a feeling that however consoling the trees might be they would not divert him from his determination that his only son should be married to this German Princess immediately.

'I just cannot do it!' the Earl exploded angrily to himself.

He climbed up the second flight of stairs towards the nursery.

When he reached the landing at the top, he opened a familiar door he had known so well ever since he could remember anything.

He had not been mistaken in what he would find.

Nanny was there, sitting in her usual chair beside the fireplace. She was knitting as the Earl expected her to be.

She looked up and, when she saw him, she gave a cry.

"Master Clive!" she exclaimed. "I heard you was comin' home!"

"Here I am, Nanny!"

He kissed her affectionately and she asked him,

"Now just what have you been up to? I was quite certain you wouldn't be comin' home unexpected like if there weren't somethin' wrong."

"You know the answer to that, Nanny," the Earl said, sitting down in the armchair opposite hers.

"In debt again?" Nanny enquired.

"Up to my neck in it!"

"That'll upset your father, Master Clive. He was cross enough at the last lot of bills he had to pay for you."

"I don't suppose you know what he has threatened me with now," the Earl asked.

"Threatened?" Nanny questioned.

"He has consulted the Queen and Her Majesty and my father are arranging that I should be forced to marry Princess Gilberta of Saxe-Coburg."

Nanny gave a gasp.

"A German? Who is she? Do you know her?"

"Of course I don't know her," the Earl replied. "She will be fat, ugly, speak extremely bad English and I speak no German."

He snapped out the words and then put his hand up to his eyes.

"For God's sake, Nanny, tell me what I can do."

Nanny was silent for a moment.

Then she said,

"I can't get over His Grace thinkin' of anythin' so wrong for you. You've been a real naughty boy in lots of ways, but I never believed he would tie you up to some woman you've never even seen and one of them foreigners at that!"

"That is what I have to do, Nanny," the Earl said, "or else Papa will not pay my bills and will cut me off without a penny which he thinks he is able to do. I may be taken to the Debtors' Prison."

Nanny gave a cry of sheer horror.

"It's wicked. It's cruel," she cried. "And I won't have that happen to my baby, indeed I won't."

She was so indignant that he just could not prevent giving a somewhat wry smile.

"I knew you would feel like that, Nanny, but I am in this mess and I have no idea how to get out of it."

He paused, sighed and then went on,

"You know what Papa is like when he sets his mind on anything. He is delighted that the Queen is helping him to trap me into matrimony."

"He's obsessed with the idea that you should have an heir," Nanny commented. "I've said to him before now, 'Master Clive'll fall in love sooner or later and then he'll give you a dozen heirs, but don't push him. No young man likes to be pushed'."

"That is true enough," the Earl said bitterly. "This is not being pushed, it is being knocked out completely in the first round before I have even had a chance to put on my boxing gloves."

"And then Her Majesty the Queen be involved too," Nanny said almost beneath her breath. "She doesn't care, because she's so unhappy, how many others are unhappy too."

"Papa has just said to me that the Princess will be compensated by becoming a Lady of the Bedchamber. I cannot see what compensation I get out of it!"

The Earl spoke with a note of misery in his voice and it made Nanny look at him piercingly.

She had loved him ever since he had been born and he had turned to her with all his troubles with his Tutors, his difficulties at school and, of course, with his father.

She thought now that she had never failed him.

She certainly could not fail him now.

But the odds had never been so heavily weighted against him.

She admitted to herself that the Duke had been very clever in obtaining the support of the Queen.

There was silence now between them.

The Earl was turning over in his mind the horror of what lay ahead of him.

"What can I do, Nanny?" he asked again. "If I go away, they will find me and anyway at the moment I have no money."

"If you went to the North Pole, they'd try and force you back," Nanny remarked.

"That is true enough," the Earl replied.

There was a note of helplessness in his voice and it almost brought tears to Nanny's eyes.

Then suddenly she gave a little cry.

"I've got it!" she exclaimed. "I knows what you must do, it's the only possible way."

CHAPTER TWO

The Earl stared at Nanny.

"What have you thought of, Nanny?" he asked.

She drew in her breath.

Then she said,

"You must elope!"

There was silence until the Earl asked,

"I don't understand, Nanny. What are you saying?"

"If His Grace thinks you've eloped, you obviously then can't be expected to marry anyone else. If you just go away and disappear, he'll search everywhere and bring you back."

"But I have no one to elope with!" he protested. "In fact, as you well know, Nanny, I have no intention of marrying anyone."

"I know that," Nanny persisted as if he was being rather stupid. "But, if you say that you'll elope and then disappear, His Grace'll think you're with someone you're goin' to marry."

"Are you suggesting I go alone?" the Earl asked as if he was finding it too difficult to understand.

"Of course I am," Nanny said. "You don't want to marry anyone and there's no reason why you should. So you tell your father you'll elope with the person you love best. It's not lyin' because it's *yourself*."

The Earl chuckled.

Nanny had always been very strict when he was a child about telling lies.

But he could see now the way that her brain was working.

"It is certainly an idea," he said slowly. "The main difficulty is, of course, that I shall have to go at once."

"At dawn tomorrow," Nanny said firmly. "And I was just thinkin' that His Grace'll expect you to go North to Gretna Green, where they'll marry you real quick."

The Earl nodded.

"In which case I will go South, in fact, I shall go all the way to Land's End to avoid Princess Gilberta!"

"That's not a bad idea, Master Clive, and I imagine it's the last place his Lordship'll think you'd go."

The Earl put his hand up to his forehead.

"Now let's think this out very carefully. I don't want to make any mistakes or I shall be in a worse mess than I am in at the moment."

"I know that," Nanny said. "So, if there's anyone you meet on the way who's interested, you say your wife's followin' you, but she's had to stop and see an ill relative or somethin' like that."

"I hope I shall meet no one, but one never knows."

"You'll need to prepare yourself," Nanny replied as if she had just thought of it. "In fact it'd be wrong for you to have a title 'cos it always attracts attention. Just be an ordinary man and, when you gets to Cornwall, you can say your wife's joinin' you as soon as she's free."

The Earl smiled.

"Who do you think I shall say it to?"

"Goodness knows!" Nanny replied, "there's enough nosey parkers in this world to fill a book, so the less people you sees the better."

Nanny was talking just the way she had when the Earl was a boy and had something special to do.

He stood up and then walked across the room to the window.

"I knew you would have some idea of how I could save myself, Nanny. But, of course, I shall miss my home and everything it means to me."

"You needn't be away for that long," Nanny said consolingly. "After all we'll keep in touch with each other and the moment that German Princess goes back to where she's come from or goes and marries someone else, you'll be free again."

"Let's hope it does not take too long," the Earl said somewhat gloomily.

"Whatever happens," Nanny added, "it's better than you being forced up the aisle with some woman you don't want. And anyway how could any man possibly be happy under those circumstances."

"That is just what I feel, Nanny, but Heaven knows what Papa will do when he hears I have gone."

There was silence for a moment before Nanny said,

"There's nothin' very much His Grace can do. If he makes a fuss about it, then the whole story'll come out as to why you've run away and that'll be the last thing he wants."

"That is true," the Earl agreed.

He turned from the window and walked back to the fireplace.

"If he thinks I have eloped and will be married, he will be forced to tell the Queen to find someone else for the Princess."

"Of course he will. Now don't upset yourself. All you have to do is to take a chaise with two of your best horses and set off for Land's End or anywhere in the South where His Grace won't be out lookin' for you."

"I was thinking of riding Crusader," the Earl said.

Nanny held up her hands.

"Now where're you goin' to put the person you've eloped with?"

The Earl laughed.

"I had forgotten that. You are quite right, Nanny, it will have to be a chaise. And I cannot take my chestnuts as they will cause too much comment."

"Now you're bein' sensible, Master Clive, and your sharp brain'll soon think the whole thing out and it'll all come quite easy."

She was talking to him, the Earl thought, just as she had done when he did not want to go back to school or when he was confronted by some problem in his lessons he did not understand.

"Now let's be sensible," Nanny said almost sharply. "You'll want money. I've just thought it'll be a good idea, to allay suspicion from anywhere you're stayin' for you to have a small case containing a woman's clothes which, of course, you says belongs to your wife."

"You think of everything, Nanny, so I will leave the case to you and I am trying to think of how I can get hold of some money. My own pockets are practically empty."

Nanny thought for a moment and then she said,

"It's Thursday today."

The Earl started.

He had not been concerned with what day of the week it was, but now he knew what Nanny meant.

On a Thursday Mr. Marshall, who was his father's secretary went to the Bank in the local town.

The people who worked in the house and on the estate were always paid their wages on Friday.

So by tonight there would be a considerable sum of money in the Estate Office where Mr. Marshall worked.

The Earl, when he was a child, had often watched him.

He arranged the money he brought back from the Bank in little piles and the Earl knew where Mr. Marshall hid the key when he left the office.

There was no need for him to tell Nanny what he was thinking as she had followed his thoughts.

"Now you sit down, Master Clive, and write a letter to your father. Tell him how sorry you are that you've gone and upset him, but at the very same time you feels you must be allowed to choose your own wife."

She paused a moment and then continued,

"Tell him you'd meant to wait a little longer, but you're now goin' to save all the trouble and fuss there'd be with a big weddin' and all the relatives chatterin', so you have decided to elope and you hopes your father'll forgive you if it distresses him."

"What will really upset him," the Earl said, "is that he cannot please the Queen. Of course she wants to make Prince Albert's cousin a Duchess, especially as my mother had Royal blood in her veins."

"Your mother, God bless her soul," Nanny said, "would never have wanted you pushed into marriage with a German woman you've never seen and that be the truth. And I'll tell His Grace to his face if I gets the opportunity!"

The Earl was standing beside Nanny, so he bent forward and kissed her cheek.

"I have never known you fail me, Nanny, when I have turned to you for help," he smiled.

"As I've said to meself," Nanny replied, "right's right and wrong's wrong and it be wrong for any man of your age to be propelled into marriage with a woman he's never seen."

"I agree with you," the Earl nodded.

He gave a sigh.

He knew that he was taking a revolutionary step. At the same time he would be alone with no one he could talk to.

He thought that it would be his father's fault if he asked Fifi to marry him.

But that would not really solve his problem as he had no wish to be married to anyone.

"I will go and write that letter to Papa," he said aloud. "And, as you think of everything, Nanny, you tell me I should take my invisible bride's clothes with me."

"If you're actin' a part," Nanny advised him, "as I've always said to you, think of every detail and make people believe what you wants them to."

The Earl remembered that this was the sort of thing Nanny had said when he was in fancy dress as a clown or a dragon for the plays he had acted in at Christmas with his cousins.

Christmas had always been a special festivity for all his family.

There had been a huge tree, presents for everyone and the children acting on a stage.

They amused a large audience that consisted of the house party and everyone who worked at The Towers both inside and out.

The Earl had always thought that it was a tradition he would carry on when he became the Duke. He would then be able to sit and admire his own children playing some fanciful part to a delighted audience.

One day that would surely happen, but he thought now that he would make absolutely certain that the mother of those children would be his own choice.

He told Nanny again how grateful he was to her.

Then he went down to his bedroom.

It was a large, very comfortable room and there was a writing table in one corner.

The Earl sat down and wrote what he thought was, on the whole, a very sensible letter to his father.

He told him he had thought over his proposition very carefully.

And it was, however, impossible for him to agree to marry a German Princess he had never met.

So he had decided that the only possible course he could take was to elope.

It would be with the person that he loved best even though until now he had not thought of doing anything so dramatic as marrying her.

"*I can only hope this unseemly haste*," he wrote, "*will not prevent me from knowing the love and happiness that you and Mama had together for so many years.*

I keep thinking that, if she was with us, she would agree with me that this is a wiser decision than the one you have made on my behalf."

He signed himself,

"*Your affectionate son,*

Clive."

Then he wrote on a postscript.

"*I know, Papa, you will understand that I had to take some money with me, because I have a very long journey to make.*"

He thought, with a smile, that would convince the Duke that he was going North to Gretna Green.

Having finished his letter he then looked round the room.

He saw that the small trunk he had brought down from London with him had not been unpacked.

He reckoned that James the footman, who usually looked after him, was waiting for his instructions.

James would not be certain whether he was staying at The Towers or returning to London tomorrow morning.

The Earl had actually brought just a few things with him down from London.

He went to the large wardrobe where all his country clothes were kept and collected a number of items that he thought he would need.

He then decided what he would wear when he left at dawn.

As it was essential not to attract any attention, he therefore chose a suit that was rather well-worn, although it had once come from a smart tailor.

He put some country shirts into the trunk and the shoes he usually wore when he was at home.

He then knew that he must go to the stables.

If he could not ride Crusader, at least he could see him.

He now thought, rather bitterly, that on the whole he minded leaving Crusader more than anyone else in his home.

The Head Groom, who had taught him to ride, was delighted to see him.

"You've bin away far too long, my Lord," he said. "We've some fine new 'orses that only you'd appreciate."

"Let me see them, Bridges," the Earl asked.

The Head Groom was only too willing to take him round. He was full of enthusiasm and compliments for the new addition of the chestnut team.

"I thought that they would please you, Bridges," the Earl said. "And, if I leave them here while I am away, I know you will look after them superbly for me."

"You can be sure of that, my Lord, though I've a pair to show you which I thinks you'll 'ave to say be as fine as them you've just bought."

He took him to a stall and the Earl saw a very well-marked white horse.

And in the next stall there was his exact twin.

"'Is Lordship purchased 'em just three weeks ago," Bridges told him, "from a man who'd just lost 'is sight and who could no longer drive 'em. As I says to 'Is Grace, they be the best purchase we've made for over a year."

"They certainly are," the Earl agreed.

He thought as he patted the horses that those were the two he would take with him tomorrow.

It might annoy his father to lose them, but then he was gaining, for the moment at any rate, the four chestnuts he had bought at Tattersalls.

He told Bridges that he now wanted to look at the travelling vehicles.

"I have a friend who is selling his," he explained, "but perhaps we have enough and so don't need anything new."

He realised that this was correct when he saw the many conveyances that his father possessed.

He knew it was one of the Duke's hobbies to have the most up to date vehicles to travel in and he had already said that nothing would induce him, unless it was totally necessary, to go by train.

"I like to be behind a horse and a good one at that," the Earl had heard him say a dozen times. "As far as I am concerned trains are ugly, noisy and smelly and I have no intention of using one!"

The Earl soon spotted the travelling chaise that he needed for his journey.

It was light, extremely well-made and, he learned from Bridges, another fairly recent purchase.

It had a good hood which could be opened and at the same time it certainly was well enough built to prevent the weather however bad from upsetting the driver.

The Earl spent a long time in the stables.

Finally, when he went back into the house, it was to find that his father had finished his tea and gone out again.

Doubtless, the Earl thought, he would be going to inspect the greenhouses or perhaps to walk in the woods again.

He therefore ate his tea quickly and went upstairs to Nanny.

"What have you been up to, Master Clive?" Nanny enquired as he came into the nursery.

"I wrote a letter to my father as you told me to," the Earl replied. "And I have chosen the horses I wish to drive and the vehicle I intend to travel in."

"Very good!" Nanny exclaimed. "I've got a case already for you with some pretty clothes that belonged to your mother and anyone who sees it'll be quite certain your wife's pretty, charming and worthy of you."

"That is exactly what I require of any woman who bears my name," the Earl smiled.

"Don't forget," Nanny said quickly, "that you must forget your present name from the moment you walks out of the house tomorrow mornin'."

"I know that," the Earl replied. "What shall I call myself?"

"Something plain, at the same time gentlemanly," Nanny suggested.

"I thought of giving myself your name," the Earl said.

As Nanny's name was Tucket, he was in fact only making a joke.

Ignoring his remark, Nanny parried,

"I was thinking of 'Stanford'. I read a book and that was what the hero was called. He always reminded me of you."

"Very well," the Earl agreed, "Stanford it shall be. Can I go on being Clive?"

"I suppose so. It's not an unusual name, but one your mother fancied."

"Clive Stanford," the Earl said. "I cannot think of anything wrong with that."

"It'll suit you all right till you comes back," Nanny replied.

"And when should that be?" the Earl enquired.

"I've been thinkin' about that. What you have to do is to let me know when you've a permanent address. Disguise your writing on the envelope so that no one in the house'll guess it be from you."

"Of course I will do that, Nanny. Then you can let me know what is happening here."

"Of course I will, Master Clive. The moment that German Princess has taken herself back to Germany where she comes from, then you can come home."

"What about my wife?" he asked.

Nanny spread out her hands.

"Use your imagination, Master Clive. She'll have to have died or perhaps found you impossible and gone home to her parents."

The Earl laughed.

"I can see that is going to be the big problem in the future, but let's not jump all our fences until we come to them."

"That's what I was thinkin'. Something'll turn up which'll make it easier, Master Clive. Anyway His Grace will not have a bride waitin' for you on your return, that's for sure."

The Earl thought that there were obviously going to be some very unpleasant moments ahead.

However, all he was concerned with was what was happening at the moment.

'The future must take care of itself,' he thought. 'In the meantime I will be free.'

Every time he thought about it he knew that it was impossible for him to endure the agony of waiting at the altar for a woman with whom he had nothing in common, a woman who had been palmed off on him by the Queen because one day he would be a Duke!

He had always known that it was going to be very difficult to find someone who loved him as a man.

At least he thought that he was conceited enough to believe that, once a young girl had met him, she would find him attractive.

Then perhaps his Social position would not be so overwhelmingly important.

'What I really want,' he told himself, 'is a woman who is really in love with me, just as if I ever do marry, it will be to a woman I love utterly and completely.'

Then he almost laughed aloud.

It was so obviously a pipe dream.

He was aware when he entered a ballroom that the Dowagers who were watching the dancers whispered when they saw him.

He knew only too well the eagerness in a mother's eyes when she had a *debutante* daughter in tow.

"How very nice to see you, Clive," she would say. "Now you must meet Alice, as she is 'coming out' this Season and we will be very hurt if you don't come to the ball we are giving for her."

If he had heard this once, he had heard it a hundred times.

He always made quite certain that he did not go to Alice's ball, although inevitably he would have a charming letter with the invitation begging him to be present.

'I suppose that one should be always grateful for small mercies,' he told himself, 'and it is impossible for me to be divided in a mother's mind from my title and, of course, Shelbourne Towers and the Dukedom.'

He loved his home, of course he did. It was one of the most beautiful houses he had ever seen.

At the same time he had often thought that it was like a millstone round his neck. It dragged him down so that he could never be free of it.

The Earl changed for dinner with the help of James the footman.

He told himself that 'Mr. Stanford' would not have such luxuries.

The bath had been brought into his bedroom and set down in front of the fireplace and then two large brass cans of hot water were poured into it.

And there was another can of cold water waiting by the fireplace if it was too hot.

James held out a large Turkish towel and the Earl rubbed himself with it when he had finished his bath.

Later on James helped him into his evening clothes and put on his shoes.

"What time does your Lordship wish to be called?" he asked.

As the Earl was dining alone with his father, he was wearing a smoking jacket.

It had become the latest fashion for men to appear in smoking jackets when there were no ladies present. It was of a dark green velvet, frogged with braid so that it looked almost military.

It was certainly more comfortable than the smart cut-away evening coat with its two pointed tails.

"Oh, call me at nine o'clock tomorrow morning," the Earl replied.

He thought by that time his father would be having breakfast and the shock of receiving his letter which he would leave on his pillow, would not be so intense as if it was earlier.

"Very good, my Lord," James nodded.

"Thank you, James," the Earl said blithely and went down the stairs to join his father with some trepidation.

He was thinking that it would be an uncomfortable dinner and to his great relief he discovered that one of his relatives had arrived at The Towers unexpectedly.

She had asked if she could stay the night.

"I am on my way to London," she explained when the Earl greeted her, "and I suspected that one of my horses was going a little lame. I therefore thought it wise to stay here if your father would have me and hope that the animal was well enough to travel on tomorrow."

The Earl was not taken in.

He had heard this sort of excuse and others much like it ever since he was a child.

It was the ambition of every relative to stay at The Towers.

They invariably had an accident near to the gates, a horse that went lame or they themselves suddenly felt faint.

Whatever it was, it assured them of a comfortable night's rest and then they somehow extorted an invitation to stay on a little longer.

The visitor this evening was a cousin of the Earl's who lived somewhere in Hampshire.

She seldom went to London, but on this occasion she had to visit a Specialist who had been recommended by her local doctor.

"What I am looking forward to," she said as they sat down to dinner, "is your wedding, Clive. I am always expecting to open a newspaper and see your engagement in the Court columns."

The Earl thought that it was just typical of one of his relatives to put her foot in it at this particular moment of time.

There was a silence round the table

Then the Duke said,

"Perhaps you will have a surprise sooner than you expect, my dear."

The cousin gave a scream of delight.

"Do you mean after all these years Clive is actually going to be married? Oh, how exciting, tell me who it is."

"I am afraid I cannot do that," the Duke replied, "because as you know there are a great number of people who have to be the first to be told of such a happy event. But I think, when you do hear the news, you will be very gratified."

"Oh Clive, how wonderful!" his cousin said turning towards him. "I am sure she is very very beautiful and will look absolutely fabulous in the Shelbourne jewels."

She then addressed the Duke.

"I remember you showing me what you had here in the safe. I was only seventeen at the time, but I have never forgotten thinking that any woman who is able to wear such glorious jewellery must be the happiest woman in the world."

The Earl did not look at his father.

He merely went on eating what was in front of him.

He only thought that, if he had to hear once again this hysteria over the Shelbourne jewels, he would give them all to a charity when he inherited the Dukedom.

"What I have to do now," his cousin was saying, "is to think of something very original but very wonderful I can give you as a wedding present. You know, Clive, we have all been saving up for it for a long time and I know that you will want something very unique and that makes it rather difficult."

"Very difficult," the Earl agreed. "So I suggest that we talk about something else."

His cousin giggled.

"I believe you are shy," she said archly. "And I do understand that this big, big secret must not be talked about until it is announced."

She raised her glass.

"I wish you, my dearest Clive, every happiness and that, I am sure, is what you will find."

There was nothing the Earl could say.

He only decided, once again, that he would avoid marriage however difficult it might be.

The whole idea of it made him feel sick.

Immediately after dinner he made an excuse to go to bed early.

"I have had a long day, Papa," he said, "and I know you will understand that I am feeling tired."

"Of course," the Duke agreed. "I am going to bed myself in a very short time. I want you to try tomorrow morning two of the new horses I have bought, so I suggest we ride, not too early, say about ten o'clock."

"That would be delightful," the Earl said.

Somewhat reluctantly the Earl kissed his cousin's cheek because she obviously expected it.

"I will not breathe a word about your secret," she whispered.

He knew from the excited note in her voice that she was longing to be in touch with their other relatives as soon as she could.

And she would tell them what they were longing to hear.

"Clive is going to be married."

"Clive is going to settle down at last."

"Now we shall have an heir to the Dukedom which is so very very important."

He could hear them saying it over and over again as he walked slowly up the stairs.

He had told James not to stay up and he did not want him to help him undress because he had no intention of doing so.

He waited until he heard his father go up to bed.

Then he opened the door of his room very quietly.

There were always a number of candles burning in the sconces, but the majority had been extinguished.

There was quite enough light, however, for him to find his way to the backstairs. There was a night footman always on duty at the bottom of the main staircase.

Then he went on to the Estate Office at the end of a long corridor.

He went in carrying a candle with him from the passage outside.

He saw that the office was exactly as he had seen it ever since he had been a child.

There was a great pile of black tin boxes at one end of it and Mr. Marshall's expansive writing table was in the centre.

Exactly opposite on the other side of the room was a safe.

It was a large safe, but also an old one.

The Earl thought, as he had thought before, that a clever burglar would have no difficulty in forcing it open.

It was something which fortunately he did not have to do, as he knew exactly where Mr. Marshall always kept the keys.

It was a secret place especially made for such a purpose in one of the drawers of his desk.

The Earl took the keys out and, crossing to the safe, opened it.

For a moment he was half-afraid that perhaps today of all days Mr. Marshall had not gone to the Bank as was his normal practice.

His fears were unfounded.

There, in the very centre of the safe was a large bag containing silver.

And another bag, not quite so large, contained gold coins.

And there was an even smaller packet for the notes.

The Earl was not certain how much he should take.

He had, however, no intention of finding himself at Land's End without any money.

If he drew a cheque from his Bank, they would at this moment expect it to be covered by his father and that meant, of course, that the Duke would know exactly where he was hiding.

After some hesitation he finally took just under one thousand pounds.

He did not believe that he would need so much as he was only journeying in the country, but equally the idea of being penniless and anonymous both at the same time was not attractive.

He filled his pockets with the gold sovereigns and some of the notes and then added just a few of the silver coins.

He then closed the safe.

Next, sitting down at the desk, he wrote a note to inform Mr. Marshall as to what he had done.

"*His Grace*," he wrote, "*will explain to you why this is necessary and I am sorry if it means another visit to the Bank tomorrow so that you are able to pay all the wages*."

He had intended to leave his note on Mr. Marshall's desk and then he had another idea.

His father would not be expecting to see him in the morning until about nine o'clock.

It would be a great mistake if Mr. Marshall came in early and the Earl was certain that he often did so.

That meant he would inform the Duke of what was happening before he had read his son's letter.

The Earl therefore opened the safe again.

He then put the note he had written to Mr. Marshall under the bag that contained the silver.

Until he picked it up he would not see that it was there.

It might even be some time before he was aware that a great deal of the money that he had brought from the Bank had gone missing.

The Earl then locked the safe, put the key back into its secret place and went up to his bedroom.

He thought it was unlikely that he would be able to sleep.

Actually he fell into a deep sleep almost at once.

*

He only woke when Nanny came into his room.

This happened just as the first rays of the sun were appearing in the East and there were still stars in the sky overhead as Nanny pulled back the curtains.

"Who is it?" the Earl asked drowsily.

Then he was aware that it was indeed Nanny.

"It's high time you were on your way," Nanny said. "So hurry up and get dressed. I've brought you a cup of tea and some slices of ham."

"You think of everything, Nanny," the Earl replied as he climbed sleepily out of bed.

"I thinks of you, Master Clive, and the sooner you be away from this house the better."

The Earl knew that she was talking sensibly.

It took him just a few minutes to put on his clothes.

Then he picked up his trunk, which was quite light, and as he did so he was aware that Nanny was carrying a case.

He knew it contained woman's clothes which were supposed to belong to his invisible wife.

"Can you manage that, Nanny?" he asked.

"I can cope with this and you too," Nanny retorted. "So come along now, Master Clive."

The Earl realised that she was more agitated than he was.

They walked quickly down the backstairs and out through a door that was close to the stables.

When they reached the stable door, the light was getting brighter.

The Earl went to the stalls where he had seen the two white horses that he had admired yesterday.

He took them out into the yard.

As he did so, he saw Nanny had woken the boy who was in charge of the stables at night.

He was rubbing his eyes as he had been asleep on a bundle of hay.

He held the horses while the Earl went to fetch the travelling chaise he had chosen for his odyssey.

It only took a few minutes for the boy to put them between the shafts as the Earl stacked his luggage into the back of the chaise.

"You've everything?" Nanny asked in a low voice. "You've not forgotten your money?"

"No, I have everything, Nanny. Don't forget me while I am away."

"I'm not likely to do that," Nanny said tartly, "with the whole household screamin' their heads off when they find out you've eloped!"

The Earl laughed.

"You can be quite certain they will!"

He put his arms round Nanny and gave her a kiss.

"You have looked after me now as you have always done," he sighed, "and I will write to you at the earliest opportunity."

"Now you take good care of yourself and don't get into any more trouble, Master Clive," Nanny ordered him as if he was still a naughty little boy.

"I will try not to," the Earl promised, "and thank you once again, Nanny. You are an angel."

"I doubts if I'll get much reward in this world or in Heaven," Nanny answered a little mournfully.

She always had the last word.

The Earl laughed again as he jumped up into the driving seat of the chaise.

The horses were fresh and responded immediately as he drove off.

He raised his hat and Nanny waved back.

Then he was speeding down the drive just as the first rays of sunshine crept up into the sky.

As he turned his horses' heads to the South, the Earl mused that this was an adventure he had not expected.

Perhaps, after all, it might not be so difficult and depressing as he feared.

The one thing that really mattered was that he was leaving behind his last chance of having to meet Princess Gilberta.

'I am free!' he now said to himself as his horses gathered speed. 'Free of being leg-shackled for the rest of my life to a German Frau.'

As he drove on, he thought that the sun seemed particularly bright.

When the horses went faster, so did his sense of excitement.

After all, this *was* an adventure!

CHAPTER THREE

The Earl drew his horses to a standstill.

He reflected with a feeling of growing triumph that he had made it.

Just ahead of him lay the County of Cornwall and after that on to Land's End.

It had taken him a long time to reach his destination but he had succeeded.

When he started off, he had little time to consider which way he should go.

All he knew was that to escape his father he would aim for Land's End and the Duke would now undoubtedly be heading to the North to look for him.

The Earl was aware that Land's End was in fact two hundred and eighty miles from London.

So then deducting the sixty miles from London to Shelbourne Towers in Oxfordshire, that had left him with a considerable mileage to travel.

It was an unknown part of England he had never had the chance to explore.

What had told him better than any signpost that he was definitely in Cornwall was when he saw the abundance of flowers everywhere.

He remembered his mother had told him years ago,

"In the very Southern parts of England, especially near Land's End, aconites bloom on the first of January and crocuses a few weeks later."

He had not been particularly interested at the time.

Now when he could see brilliant colourful flowers in every direction, he felt that Cornwall must surely be a Fairyland.

There was endless myrtle and veronica, bamboos, rhododendrons and hydrangeas all in the open air.

The colours seemed to mingle with the blue of the sky and it was difficult to know where the earth stopped and the Heavens began.

To his surprise he had enjoyed every moment of his drive to Cornwall. It was hard to believe but it had taken him nearly five weeks.

When he had set out, he expected it to be a bore and strangely enough it was never that.

First of all he enjoyed driving alone, finding a chit-chatty conversation prevented him from concentrating on his horses.

He thought when he left Shelbourne Towers behind that he would find the evenings heavy going.

Instead he had found that they were amusing and interesting and also they were something new which he had never expected to find.

He had been wise enough to avoid the Posting inns and hotels.

He had concentrated on finding small villages with the usual black and white inn on the village green.

Inevitably there was a pond on which there were ducks and usually small boys throwing stones.

He had been careful to choose inns which looked clean if somewhat primitive.

He would settle his horses into makeshift stables at the back of the inns making sure that they had fresh straw and good food to eat and then he could think about himself.

For the first two weeks the food problem had been solved by Nanny.

She had suggested that he put in two sacks of the very best oats, which was what the horses in the stables at home enjoyed.

And that at least saved some of his money.

The inns themselves were cheap, usually clean and welcoming.

What he found interesting as ordinary Mr. Stanford was that the publican and his wife, if he had one, talked to him as if he was an old friend.

They told him their difficulties and their triumphs and how they kept themselves going however hard it was at times.

Sometimes, when he was talking to them after an edible if not particularly exciting meal, they were joined by the village elders who came in for a glass of ale.

They usually sat on the hard bench outside the inn and what they had to say to him the Earl found extremely interesting.

He heard the whole truth about the aristocracy of the neighbourhood and he understood why they despised a man who did not give value for money to those who paid him.

The Earl had always been at his ease with the men he commanded when he was in the Regiment.

Of course it was impossible to forget that he was an Officer and they were just serving soldiers.

However, it was different now because he was not smartly dressed and was staying at an inn.

Those who came there to drink with the publican and his wife treated him as an equal.

When he realised that this could be an advantage, he was careful not to say that he owned his two superb horses.

They naturally attracted a great deal of favourable attention and he explained that he was running them in for their owner.

Of all the places he stayed at, he never came up against one inn he disliked or where he was afraid of being cheated.

There was only one occasion when he was nervous.

It was when he was nearing his destination.

Some men came into the inn after he had finished his evening meal and just as soon as he saw them he was suspicious.

There were six of them and the Earl was almost certain that he was right in thinking they were smugglers or thieves of some sort.

They talked in low voices amongst themselves.

Then listening, while pretending not to do so, the Earl thought that he heard them mention his horses.

They had, of course, seen them when they put their own into the inn's stable.

Without appearing to be in any haste, the Earl had finished his meal.

Leaving the room where he was eating, he talked for some minutes with the publican, who was still doling out drinks in the bar.

The Earl then sauntered casually over the courtyard at the back of the inn.

His father who was frightened of highwaymen had sensibly placed a pistol in all his carriages and vehicles.

When revolvers were invented the Duke substituted the latest addition for the old-fashioned pistol and it was kept just by the driver's seat in a special place where it could not be seen.

The driver had, in fact, only to put down his hand to pick up the weapon if it was required and in most cases he would be too swift for the highwayman who was trying to rob him.

The Earl bent over the chaise and instantly found the secret place where the revolver was hidden.

He did it all very cleverly and he was almost certain that no one was watching him.

Yet he was taking no chances.

Then he went into the stable with his horses.

He had been very careful not to drive them too far each day and he gave them plenty of time to rest at every place he stayed the night.

The Earl saw now that they were lying down. They had eaten their oats and drunk a great deal of the fresh water he had put into their buckets.

The Earl then sat down on a pile of fresh straw that was stacked at the end of the stable.

He waited.

It was an hour before the men who had entered the inn came out into the yard.

Their horses were at the end of the stable and there were actually two stalls empty between the Earl's horses and theirs.

As the first man came into the stable, he did not go into the stall opposite him.

He walked along to where the Earl had put his two horses.

It was then that the Earl rose without appearing to hurry from the straw he had been sitting on.

Picking up an armful of it he carried it towards the stall where one of his horses was resting.

In doing so he came face to face with the man who he thought was a smuggler.

He was undoubtedly in some trade or business that the authorities would not approve of.

"Be that your 'orse?" the man asked.

"I wish it was," the Earl replied. "The pair belong to someone so important I dare not take my eye off them."

"They be nice animals," the man commented.

There was a note in his voice that made the Earl tighten his fingers round the revolver hidden in the straw.

"All I can tell you," he said in a confidential tone, "that if anything happens to either of these two horses there would be an uproar in this County that would take the roof off."

He saw the man was listening to him intently and he then went on,

"They are the apple of their owner's eye and he has said to me a dozen times that if anything happens to those horses, 'I will strangle you and anyone else who damages them'."

The Earl spoke in quite a ferocious tone, so much so that the smuggler took a step back.

He looked at the horse nearest to him once again and then turned away.

"I don't envy you your job," he said. "It sounds dangerous."

"That is putting it lightly," the Earl replied, "and the sooner that I can take these horses back to where they belong the better I shall be pleased."

The man went back to his friends and they had a whispered conversation.

Although the Earl could not hear it, he was certain that the man was telling his comrades that it was not worth the risk.

Two of the men shrugged their shoulders and then they collected their own horses and rode off.

It was not until the Earl saw the last man leaving the courtyard that he slipped his revolver back into his pocket.

He was putting down the straw that he was holding when the publican joined him.

"Them men didn't give you any trouble?" he asked.

"I think they might have done," the Earl replied, "but after what I told them they thought better of it."

The publican gave a sigh of relief.

"I were afraid that they might want to take your 'orses," he said. "They've a bad reputation in the County, but most people be too frightened to give evidence against 'em."

"Do you think they will come back?" the Earl asked him.

The publican shook his head.

"I'd be surprised if they does. They were on their way to Exeter and I 'opes we've 'eard the last of 'em."

"I hope so too for your sake. Those sort of men are no blessing to anyone."

"That be true enough," the publican agreed. "Now come and 'ave a drink and, because I'm glad they've gone without causin' us no trouble, I'll stand you an ale."

The Earl accepted it graciously.

As he went to bed, he reflected that he had had a narrow escape.

Stealing horses was a well-known trick amongst a certain type of traveller.

He had heard stories of how in quite a respectable inn a newcomer with a well-bred horse would be surprised at the friendliness of some of the other diners.

They would offer him drink after drink which he was then foolish enough to accept and it was only when the morning came round did he find that his good horse had disappeared.

In its place was an old half-starved animal which was quite useless.

When the Earl walked up the stairs to his bed, he thought that he was very stupid.

He should have thought of bringing a revolver with him.

He was only very thankful that his father had had the foresight to give the order that every vehicle belonging to The Towers was to be armed.

'Things are always different to what one expects,' the Earl thought. 'I am learning on this trip quite a lot I did not know before.'

However, there were no other unpleasant incidents.

In fact he usually left the small inn where he had stayed feeling that he had made new friends and, although he would never see them again, they would never forget him.

It was quite unnecessary for him to say anything about his wife.

He was accepted as a traveller and the people he talked to were too polite to be over-curious.

Once they learnt that he was earning his living by looking after horses they then told him of the difficulties of getting a job or how lucky they had been in working for a man who paid them fairly.

It was a very different situation, the Earl thought, to what was happening in the towns.

There men were expected to work for what was often a pittance or go hungry.

It was difficult in the beauty of Cornwall to worry and the Earl could only think that the people living in such lovely surroundings must be happy.

He remembered one of his Tutors telling him that Cornwall was the foot of England, the Lizard the heel and Land's End the toe.

Now it was something he could see for himself.

He wished he had paid more attention to his history and geography lessons when they were concerned with his own country.

What he did recall was that Cornwall had always been famous for its minerals.

Solomon had wanted to emphasise his glory and it was said that he had carried away from Cornwall tin and other metals for the building of his Temple in Jerusalem.

The first inn at which the Earl stayed in Cornwall was just over the border from Devon.

The publican told him that for centuries the toast at all the local gatherings was for 'fish, tin and copper.'

However, the Earl did not expect to be concerned with any of these things.

He was making for Penzance and he understood that it was the nearest town to Land's End.

The weather since he left home had been extremely good and only twice had he been forced to put up the hood of his chaise.

Now there was a cloudless blue sky above him with exquisitely coloured flowers on each side of him.

He deliberately avoided main roads where possible.

Then he turned down a rather narrow lane where there were lofty trees on one side of the road and like everywhere else there was a profusion of flowers.

He was going slowly because the sun was warm and he was bareheaded and enjoying its warmth.

Suddenly, as he turned a corner, he saw that there was what was called a gig in Oxfordshire and there sitting in the driving seat was a woman.

It was impossible to pass her and the Earl was just about to call out for her to move her cart.

Then he could see standing by the gig the woman was driving was a man.

As the Earl sharply drew his horses to a standstill, the man looked up.

To the Earl's surprise he was wearing a mask.

Swiftly with a quickness which was inherited, the Earl put down his hand for the revolver.

He had put it back into its secret place in the chaise.

Even as he grasped the revolver, he realised that the highwayman was removing the horse from the woman's carriage.

He was now drawing a pistol from his belt. He had placed it there while he was unfastening the horse from the shafts.

The Earl's years in the Army had taught him to act quickly.

He fired the revolver over the highwayman's head and shouted,

"Go or you will have the next one in your throat!"

The highwayman's jaw dropped.

Then quicker than seemed possible he sprang onto the back of his horse that was standing a little way in front of the gig.

The highwayman rode off at a pace that could have made him the winner on any Racecourse!

As he disappeared amongst the trees, the Earl put his revolver back into its secret place.

Then he tied up his horses' reins and climbed out of the chaise.

He walked over to the gig and said to the woman who was still sitting there,

"Are you alright?"

She turned her head and he saw that she was young and exceptionally pretty.

At the same time she was pale with fear and her eyes were frightened.

"Thank you – thank you," she managed to say in a broken little voice. "He was taking away – my horse."

"I saw that," the Earl said.

He walked to the front of the gig and saw that the horse, which was well-bred, was apparently unperturbed by what had been occurring.

The highwayman had loosened one of the shafts of her gig and the Earl put it back into place.

The reins were lying limply on the horse's back and he handed them to the girl.

"You have had a lucky escape," the Earl said. "Do you have many highwaymen in this part of the world?"

"I have not met one – before," the girl answered in a soft mellow voice. "But, of course – I have read about them in the newspapers. But then I did not think it would ever happen – to me."

The Earl smiled.

"A great number of people think like that and you should have something with you to protect yourself."

"I did not think of it," the girl replied, "and I know that my father will be extremely angry – when he hears that a highwayman should dare to stop me."

"You sound as if you are very important locally," the Earl said with a smile.

The girl gave a little laugh.

"Not me, but my father – "

"Well, tell your father that it is dangerous for young ladies to drive about alone," the Earl said. "There are far too many thieves all over the world wanting a better horse than they have themselves."

"Perhaps that is true where you come from," the girl replied. "Here in Cornwall we have smugglers and we are quite used to them. But, as I have said, I have never – encountered a highwayman before."

"I expect like everyone else," the Earl said, "you will never learn and this is indeed an uncomfortable way of experiencing the truth."

The girl laughed.

"I was very frightened, and thank you so much for saving me. I know that my father will want to thank you too."

"As you live in this part of the country," the Earl asked, "can you recommend a quiet inn somewhere near Land's End."

"There are hotels in Penzance," the girl replied.

"I am sure of that," the Earl answered. "But I really prefer a quiet village inn where, if possible, I am the only visitor."

"I can understand you feeling like that, but here they are few and far between. After what has happened, you must be careful with your beautiful horses."

"I have been all the time I have been coming here," the Earl replied.

Now the girl was looking at his horses and she said,

"They are certainly a magnificent pair and perfectly matched. Do they belong to you?"

The Earl thought that it was wise to stick to the story he had told so far.

"I just wish they did. I am running them in for their owner."

The girl looked at him before she asked,

"Do you mean he employs you?"

"You could put it like that. But it is work that I really enjoy."

There was silence for a moment and then the girl said,

"My Papa is looking for someone to help us in the stables. We are shorthanded at the moment because our Head Groom, who has been with us many years, has died. We want someone who really understands horses and loves them."

The Earl was amused.

It was the first time in his life he had been offered the job of what he supposed was the post of a superior and trusted servant.

"There is a very nice cottage," the girl went on. "It is not very big, but comfortable with plenty of room for two people."

"Are you suggesting," the Earl questioned, "that I should now apply to your father for the position of Head Groom?"

"I was just mentioning that was what we require," the girl replied. "And, as you have been so kind and saved me, I know that Papa would want to show his gratitude in some way."

She paused, but, as the Earl did not say anything, she went on,

"If you are not interested, the least we can do is to put you up for the night."

"Thank you," the Earl answered. "My horses have done quite enough travelling for one day and I never push them too hard. So I would be most grateful if I could find accommodation without going too much further."

"Then if you will follow me," the girl said. "My home is only about two miles away."

She was lifting her reins when the Earl suggested,

"I think perhaps we should introduce ourselves and you have not yet told me the name of your father."

"How silly of me," she replied. "He is General Sir Aubin Wymond and most Cornish people are very proud of him."

The Earl thought vaguely that he had indeed heard the name mentioned before, but it would, however, be a mistake to say so.

Aloud he said,

"My name is Stanford – Clive Stanford."

The girl smiled and it was a very pretty smile.

"My name," she responded, "is Melva Wymond."

"Now that we are introduced," the Earl said, "I will follow you as you suggest and at least my horses will be safe for tonight."

"When that awful man intended to take Dragonfly away from me," Melva said, "I was terrified, but I could not think what I could do."

"There was nothing you could do," the Earl replied. "Except pray for a miracle and that I feel is exactly what did happen."

"Yes, it did!" Melva exclaimed. "You came down from Heaven as if you were the Archangel Gabriel when I thought that I would lose my Dragonfly for ever."

"I think it would be a mistake," the Earl suggested, "until we can be really certain that this man has either left the neighbourhood or been put in prison, for you to drive about alone."

He almost added,

'You are far too pretty for one thing.'

Then he thought it might sound rather too familiar for someone who was seeking employment.

There was no doubt, however, that Melva was as pretty as the flowers that were growing all round them.

From what he could see of her hair under her hat he knew that it was as golden as the sunshine and her skin was the pink and white of the musk roses.

'I have most certainly chosen someone particularly lovely for my good deed,' he thought, as he climbed back into the chaise.

Melva had now driven Dragonfly forward and was moving slowly down the lane.

The Earl followed, thinking that this was something he had not expected.

It was another intriguing incident to add to those he had already experienced.

'What I shall have to do,' he thought, 'is to write a book of what has happened on this journey. I had certainly not expected to intimidate a highwayman and, combined with the smugglers and whatever else may still happen, it will certainly keep a reader interested and amused.'

Melva quickened the pace a little as the lane grew wider.

Next there were several small thatched cottages that the Earl thought must be part of a village and then he saw a Church at the end of the road.

Just moments later, before they reached the Church, there were some impressive-looking gates.

Melva went through them.

There were trees, with the sun streaming through their leaves, whose branches almost made a roof over the drive.

At the very end of the long drive there was a very attractive house.

It was obviously very old yet it had the comfortable look of having been well-preserved over the ages.

The Earl guessed it was what was called a Manor House and he was certain that it had been built in Tudor times.

The garden was a mass of flowers and shrubs in bloom.

The Earl could only look at his surroundings with interest as Melva drove on past the house and through an archway.

This was also of Tudor bricks and led straight into a cobbled stable yard.

A young groom came out of one of the buildings and went straight to the head of Dragonfly.

As the Earl then brought his horses to a standstill, Melva, who had stepped down from the gig, came to his side.

"I am afraid," she said, "that, as we are very short-handed, you will have to put your horses into their stalls yourself. One of our boys has gone to Penzance today and the other one is not very intelligent."

"I will manage it," the Earl smiled. "It is what I usually do anyway."

"I thought that you might say that," Melva replied. "Now I will show you where you can find some food for your horses."

As she was speaking to him, the Earl was already unfastening one of his horses from the shaft.

Melva did the other and she then led the one she had released and the Earl followed her.

He was glad to see that the stables, although they looked old, were large and comfortable and there was fresh straw in the stalls and plenty of fresh water.

There was, he realised, quite a number of horses in the stables and he had the idea that there were others across the yard in a paddock.

As if she was reading his thoughts, Melva said,

"I am afraid that we have many more horses than grooms at the moment. If you could help Papa, he would be extremely grateful."

"I think I will be grateful too," the Earl replied.

She smiled at him.

He realised that she was delighted to think that he might be available.

"The cottage is over there," she said, pointing to the end of the yard. "It is very pretty and was built at the same time as the house. One of my father's relations lived in it for some years."

The Earl was wondering whether he could manage a cottage on his own and again, as if she knew what he was thinking, Melva said,

"If you don't want to cook for yourself and clean the place, I am sure that we could find a woman from the village to help you. It is actually men we are short of at the moment, not women."

"That sounds a good idea," the Earl replied. "As it happens my wife should be with me, but she has been held up by the illness of one of her family. She may be joining me later, but I would certainly appreciate some help until she does."

"Come and tell Papa how you saved me," Melva answered, "and how I think I have found someone to look after the horses. That will please him very much."

As she spoke, she looked questioningly at the Earl as if she thought that he might back out at the last moment.

"Whatever happens," he said, "I am very grateful to have a bed for the night. And, as I have no wish to go into Penzance, I certainly would not want to encounter your highwayman friend again unexpectedly."

"I think if he does see you, he will run away again," Melva said. "He did not expect to find a man threatening him with a revolver whilst he himself was doing all the intimidating. I expect he has done it to dozens of helpless people."

"I am sure he has," the Earl replied. "That is why you must never take any risks in the future."

He was thinking that it was ridiculous to allow such a pretty girl to wander about the countryside without an escort.

Also she was apparently without any way of being able to protect herself and, as her father was a soldier, he should know better than that.

They walked in through the front door.

The house inside was just as attractive as the Earl had expected. The rooms had low ceilings, but were large and comfortable and much of the furniture seemed to be as historic as the house itself.

They passed through a large hall and then through several rooms that seemed to connect with each other.

Next they came to a room at the back of the house that had large long windows overlooking the garden. They had diamond shaped panes that glittered invitingly in the setting sun.

As soon as they entered, the Earl knew at once why the General had made this his sitting room.

The walls were all covered with books and ancient maps of strange parts of the world.

There were also some fine pieces of carving that could only have come from the East.

The General was a very good-looking man who had obviously been very handsome in his youth.

Whatever hair he had left was turning white and the Earl guessed that he was getting on for sixty.

It did, however, seem a little strange that he should have such a young daughter.

For the moment the Earl was slightly worried in case he had met Sir Aubin before, in which case he would know who he was.

Melva had run across the room to kiss her father, who was sitting at a writing table in the window.

"I have had – such a terrible experience, Papa," she began breathlessly. "A highwayman was trying to steal – Dragonfly when this kind man saved me."

"A highwayman! What are you talking about?" Sir Aubin enquired. "There are no highwaymen here."

"There was a very nasty one," Melva said, "and he was just taking Dragonfly – from between the shafts when Mr. Stanford came round the corner with his team and – threatened him with a revolver."

The General rose from his chair and held out his hand to the Earl.

"If you saved my daughter and her horse," he said, "I am in your debt and very grateful indeed."

"There is a chance, if I had come a few moments later," the Earl replied, "the man would have undoubtedly got away and left his own horse behind, which was not a good exchange."

"I can hardly believe it!" the General exclaimed. "We have not had a highwayman in this part of the world for years."

"There is most definitely one here at the moment," Melva said. "And I am not going out alone unless you give me a revolver."

The General sat down and indicated a chair to the Earl.

"Sit down and tell me exactly what happened," he proposed.

"Before you do that," Melva intervened, "I have found out that Mr. Stanford is looking for a position with horses. You should see the pair he is driving, Papa. I am trying to persuade him to help us."

The General's eyes lit up.

"We are desperately short-handed at the moment. I have two men coming from Penzance to see me tomorrow, but I don't think that either of them is very experienced."

"What I really asked your daughter to do," the Earl said, "was to recommend a quiet inn where I could stay the night. I am always worried about having my horses stolen, as they are an exceptionally fine twin pair. I am breaking them in for their owner."

"He might be persuaded to stay and help us for a little while," Melva chipped in.

"Then that is just what I am going to suggest," the General said. "And I must thank you again for saving my daughter from a very unpleasant experience and her horse from being stolen."

"I think the Police should be notified that such a man is in the neighbourhood," the Earl suggested. "Once these highwaymen get their hands on a good horse, they either sell it or else treat it so badly that it does not have a very long life."

The General nodded his head.

"I have heard that too. But do tell me a little about yourself, Stanford. How is it that you know so much about horses?"

"I have always had a great deal to do with them," the Earl answered. "And I was in a Cavalry Regiment."

"Which one was that?" the General asked.

The Earl thought that it would be a mistake for him to say that he had been in the Household Cavalry.

So he therefore replied,

"The Ninth Queen's Royal Lancers, General."

"I know them, yes, of course, I know them," the General said. "A very fine Regiment. Why did you leave the Army?"

"I was in India for a short time," the Earl replied, which was the truth. "But, as I wanted to come back to England to be with my family, I resigned."

"You said you have a wife," Melva asked, "have you any children?"

"Not yet," the Earl answered.

Melva turned to her father.

"What I promised Mr. Stanford," she said, "is that, if he comes to us, we will find someone to look after him until his wife arrives. I am sure, like all men, he dislikes cooking and worst of all having to clean the house."

"That is true," the Earl smiled, "and I would be very grateful for any help I can have."

"We will find you someone," the General replied. "Women are two a penny round here, but men are hard to find."

"If you ask me they are far too busy smuggling," Melva said. "I saw in the newspapers that some smugglers have been caught, but in some mysterious way they cannot find the large amount of wine that they stole from a French ship."

"That is an old story," the General remarked.

"I have already heard that Cornwall is famous for its smugglers," the Earl commented.

"It is something we are not at all proud about," the General replied. "And the sooner we stop it the better. Now let's talk a little business and I suggest, Melva, you go and fetch Mr. Stanford a glass of ale. I think that it is something he deserves after what he has done."

"Perhaps he would rather prefer a glass of claret," Melva said. "I should be crying my eyes out now if he had not come along at exactly the right moment."

The General made a gesture with his hands.

"The choice is yours, Stanford."

"I am delighted to accept a glass of claret," the Earl said.

Melva went towards the door.

"If I was a smuggler," she piped up, "I would bring you a case or a barrel of it. But as it is, I can only thank you once again."

She was gone before the Earl could reply,

Then the General said,

"I must add my gratitude to my daughter's. It was very lucky that you came by before the horse was actually stolen."

"It was lucky for you, General," the Earl answered, "but it was also lucky for me. I shall be very grateful to be allowed to spend a little time looking after your horses."

"I realise that you will want help. I have these two men coming tomorrow, but that is about all."

"I expect I can manage, General."

"I have a feeling," the General said slowly, "that this would be something new to you. Have you been in employment of this sort since you left the Army?"

The Earl thought quickly.

He realised that the General was astute enough and too experienced to be deceived.

He was obviously by now well aware that he was a gentleman and that he had not been employed as a senior servant previously.

Thinking quickly the Earl said after a moment,

"Things have been rather difficult for me recently. They are entirely family matters, which I would rather not discuss. But if you will employ me for the moment, I will make sure that you do not regret it."

"I rather thought it must be something like that," the General said. "And I am at this very moment, like my daughter, much in need of help."

"Then if we can leave it at that, General, I can only promise to do my best and hope I will not disappoint you."

The General smiled at him.

"I think that is not likely," he said. "I have had a long experience of men, as you can imagine, and I always know whether a man is telling the truth or not."

Before the Earl could reply, Melva came back into the room.

She was carrying a tray on which there were three glasses and a bottle of claret.

"Here you are, Papa," she said. "It's your very best claret, but can we offer Mr. Stanford anything else after he has been so kind and brave?"

“You are quite right,” the General agreed, “so pour us all a glass.”

CHAPTER FOUR

The Earl took his horse up to the jump.

It rose without any hesitation and landed perfectly.

As the jump was decidedly higher than it had been the previous morning, the Earl was pleased.

The horse he was riding was one of the best in the General's collection.

Then he drew the horse to a standstill and turned round to watch Melva.

He realised that she was an exceptional rider.

He was, however, slightly worried at the moment because she was following him over the jump he had just taken.

And this, he thought, was too high for a woman.

But she had insisted and he gave in.

He watched her riding up to it, thinking that the way she sat on a horse was superlative.

Then, as her mount quickened its pace, he almost held his breath as Melva took the jump.

He need not have been concerned.

The horse cleared it with inches to spare and landed as well as his mount had done.

As Melva rode towards him, he saw a flush in her cheeks and the excitement in her eyes.

"I did it!" she exclaimed.

"I watched you," the Earl replied, "and it was quite perfect."

"Papa will be very pleased that this horse is doing so well," Melva said. "He rather doubted when he bought it if it was as good as its owner claimed."

"I think we can tell him it is outstanding. Now we have two superb horses and that should easily be enough for anyone."

Melva laughed.

"Not for Papa. He wants his whole stables to be good enough to win every steeplechase. But I think that these two will certainly win the one he has entered for next month."

"Are you going to ride one?" the Earl asked rather sharply.

He found it difficult when he looked at Melva not to feel afraid of what she might do next.

She was so small and had a very fragile appearance about her and it made him anxious every time she took any risk or even thought about it.

He was beginning to realise, however, that she was actually extremely strong.

She also had what is the envy of all good riders, an instinct.

It made her not ask more of a horse than it was capable of doing.

The Earl had ridden with many women, but he had never known anyone quite as good as Melva and she was so unselfconscious about it.

She listened to all his instructions most respectfully and seldom argued with him.

Moreover, he was beginning to realise that she only insisted on taking on some particular jump when she knew that there was no danger in it.

Either for herself or the horse she was riding.

As the horses they were riding on now had to be exercised, they set off at a sharp gallop.

They were on the flat ground in front of The Manor House and it was brilliant with bright flowers of every description.

The Earl thought to himself that nothing could be more beautiful except the girl riding beside him.

The more he saw of Melva the more he knew that she was wasting her sublime beauty here in Cornwall.

As he had learned from the General, there were few neighbours and even less young, who would be Melva's contemporaries.

The General had realised that the Earl was not what he pretended to be and he had therefore suggested the first night he arrived that he should dine with them.

"Tomorrow," the General said, "we will arrange for some woman from the village to look after you, but I doubt if she will be a very good cook."

Their dinner, the Earl found, was exceptional.

He learned that the General in his retirement liked his comforts.

There was a butler and two footmen to wait on them and he was to find out later that there were three in the kitchen.

What was missing, the Earl now told himself, were friends.

They should be sitting round the table enjoying the excellent *cuisine* and the even more excellent wines as well as stimulating and scintillating conversation with a number of locals of varying ages.

Melva did not complain.

All she did say the first morning after she and the Earl had ridden together was,

"Thank you very much, Mr. Stanford. It is lovely having someone to ride out with. I sometimes feel lonely when I go out by myself."

"You don't take a groom with you?" the Earl asked.

The young women he had met either in London or the country would never have ridden alone. If there was no relation or friend to accompany them, then they would be followed by a groom.

Melva shook her head.

"The two boys we have already are quite good at cleaning and feeding the horses, but they are not riders."

The Earl supposed it was safe enough in Cornwall, but after their experience with the highwayman he thought that they should be especially careful.

At least until the man was either arrested or had left the County.

On the General's instructions a groom had taken a note to the Chief Constable.

He lived just outside Penzance and sent a message to say that he would do what he could to arrest the man.

*

The Earl was busy in the next few days.

He found that the two new men the General had engaged from Penzance were efficient at looking after the horses.

They kept the stables clean and tidy, but they were, however, not naturals with the animals.

Having watched them exercising two of the horses he decided that was what he and Melva must do and the grooms should stay on the ground.

The General rode every morning before breakfast and alone.

"I dislike talking to anyone early in the morning," he explained, "and, when I am riding, I can make plans in my mind which I follow for the rest of the day."

There were many things for him to do on the estate.

He was also, the Earl learned, writing his memoirs of his time in the Army.

As he had enjoyed a very distinguished career and received every honour it was possible to obtain, the Earl had thought it was likely to be a particularly interesting book and he would like to read it.

To write it the General would shut himself up in his study and forbid anyone to disturb him.

The Earl thought it must be rather dismal for Melva to be alone with no one to talk to.

She certainly enjoyed riding with him and she was excited at the idea of building jumps in what they called 'the paddock'.

The Earl made them a little higher for the horses every day and then he had to admit that they responded gallantly.

The first night when he had dined with the General and Melva he had worn his green smoking jacket. It was the only evening clothes he had put in his luggage.

After that it was taken for granted that his meals would be in the dining room.

The General talked to him about the Army and the wars and battles that he had been involved in.

The Earl found it all very interesting.

He also thought that Melva, in the simple evening gown she wore, looked very lovely.

It seemed extraordinary, he reflected, that she had remained undiscovered, one might say, here in the depths of Cornwall.

In London she would most certainly have been an undoubted success.

She did not interrupt when her father and the Earl were talking, but she listened intently to everything that was said.

And when she was riding with the Earl the next day she asked what he thought were most intelligent questions.

*

On the fourth day when they rode together, he said to her,

"What do you intend to do with yourself, Melva? You can hardly spend the rest of your life here at the end of nowhere."

Melva grinned.

"Is that what it seems to you? I suppose it is rather like a desert island, but I love our home, I love my father and I love our horses."

"That may be enough at the moment," the Earl said. "But you will want to get married one day and where are the suitors?"

Melva laughed loudly.

"I expect they will come up out of the ground or arrive in a smuggler's ship!"

She gave a sideways glance before she said,

"Or perhaps a highwayman holding me up on the road!"

"That was not a joke," the Earl said. "If I had not come along the lane at that particular moment, he would have undoubtedly stolen Dragonfly and perhaps assaulted you."

"He could not insult me more," Melva said, "than by attempting to steal my Dragonfly."

It was not what the Earl had meant, but he thought it best not to explain any further.

"You must understand," he said, "you are never in the future to go out riding without someone else with you and never, never to drive alone along these deserted lanes without a groom."

"That is an easy instruction to follow at this very moment," Melva said. "But grooms come and go and I can hardly stay in the house all day with nothing to do except read, read, read."

"I thought you enjoyed reading," the Earl quizzed her.

"I do," she answered, "I love books. At the same time I want to ask questions about what I have read. I want to talk to someone and, if there is no one in the house apart from Papa who is locked in his study, I have to go out looking for friends."

"They should come looking for you," the Earl said firmly.

"Then you will have to tell them so," she retorted. "But at the moment look how lucky I am to have you."

"I shall not be staying with you for ever," the Earl said quietly.

Melva looked at him quickly.

"You are not thinking of leaving us?"

"Not at the moment," the Earl replied, "but I have my future to think of just as you have yours."

"If you go away now, Papa will be very upset. He said to me only last night after you had gone to bed that I was very lucky to have found you and he had never before felt so happy about his horses."

The Earl thought this was the sort of compliment he liked.

However he was waiting anxiously for a letter from Nanny.

As soon as he had arrived at The Manor House, he had written to her giving his address.

He had told her that he had enjoyed the drive and had only stayed one night in each place until he was where he was now.

"I have obtained a job of looking after horses," he wrote, *"with a charming retired General and his daughter, who is one of the best riders I have ever seen.*

This is a very beautiful but lonely place and I shall be longing to receive your news as to what is happening at home."

He had expected that the post would take some time to deliver his letter to The Towers.

The days seemed to pass by slowly when there was no reply.

Then, when he had come down to breakfast early this morning, he had seen a letter.

It was lying in the hall where the postman had left it amongst several others for the General.

The Earl, who was now on his way to the stables, opened the envelope eagerly with Nanny's writing on it.

She had written her to him on cheap unheaded writing paper and she must have had it up in the nursery for many years.

Her handwriting, although not particularly elegant, had always been easy to read.

The Earl read,

"Dearest Master Clive,

I was so glad to get your letter and hear you'd reached Cornwall safely.

There was a terrible commotion here when His Grace found out you'd gone.

He went into one of his towering rages and sent Mr. Marshall's assistant immediately by train to Gretna Green with orders to stop your marriage and insist you return home immediately.

His Grace then cross-examined everyone in the house, including me, to find out if you'd said where you'd be likely to be going and who with.

Of course he learnt nothing and that made him angrier still.

When Mr. Jenkins comes back from Gretna Green saying there was no sign of you, His Grace didn't believe him and made him return immediately in case you'd turned up after he'd gone.

In the meantime I rather thinks he had discussed it all with the Chief Constable, who's been here several times and I guess, although I don't know, he's had nothing to tell him."

The Earl gave a sigh of relief before he read on,

"*After a fortnight had gone by, His Grace were forced to go to Windsor Castle.*

I understands he told the Queen you'd gone abroad unexpected-like and therefore he couldn't do a thing about bringing you to Windsor Castle till you comes back."

The Earl smiled when he read this.

Then he turned over the page to see that Nanny had continued,

"*Mr. Barker has been told by Mr. Wilkins that Princess Gilberta be quite a pretty girl and not so fat and heavy as you suspected her would be.*"

The Earl knew that Wilkins was his father's valet and he would have gone with him to Windsor Castle.

Nanny went on,

"*At the same time Mr. Wilkins says he didn't think the Princess were good enough for you and it were lucky that you couldn't be found as her doesn't speak very much English.*"

'I thought that would be the case,' the Earl said to himself, feeling rather smug that he had been right.

He turned to the last sheet of Nanny's letter.

"*His Grace has been in London for this last week, although he can't be expecting to find you there.*

I thinks you're quite safe if you stays put where you are a bit longer.

Take care of yourself, Master Clive, and I'll write again as soon as there's any more news.

Yours affectionately

Nanny."

The Earl read the letter through twice.

He could easily understand what a commotion he must have caused and his father would have been furious and screaming at everyone.

Equally he could only thank Heaven that he had escaped, otherwise he would be now, at this very moment, at Windsor Castle meeting the German Princess.

After that it was only a question of time before he was married and in his opinion imprisoned for life.

He put the letter into his pocket and went on to the stables.

Melva was there looking very attractive in a riding skirt and muslin blouse.

It was what she wore every morning and, as there was no one to see her, she did not wear a hat. As it was so warm, she wore no jacket either.

As the Earl arrived, one of the men was bringing Dragonfly out of the stables.

The Earl raised his eyebrows.

"Is it Dragonfly's turn today?" he asked.

Melva gave him a sideways glance.

"You were not here to give the orders, so I am giving Dragonfly a treat."

"I wanted you to ride Black Prince," the Earl said.

Melva looked at him beseechingly.

"Let me take him out this afternoon. I just cannot disappoint Dragonfly now he is saddled and I do love him more than any of the other horses."

She was pleading with the Earl.

He picked her up and placed her on Dragonfly's saddle.

As he did so, she was so light that she seemed to fly onto the horse.

"Thank you," Melva breathed, "I am very grateful."

"They are your horses," the Earl pointed out, "and, of course, you can ride whichever one you wish to. At the same time we have promised your father to improve them all and there are only you and I to do it for him."

"But then look how clever we are," Melva replied laughingly.

The Earl went into the stables to choose his own horse to ride.

He thought as he did so that he must find someone to take his place when he left and it would be a crime to let these splendid horses down when he had done so much for them already.

The stable boys, keen and enthusiastic though they might be, were just not good enough to do what he and Melva were doing.

He then chose a horse for himself that he thought needed more training than the rest.

He hurried after Melva who was on her way to the paddock.

She looked at his horse and exclaimed,

"So you have chosen Red Star. I knew he would have to be dealt with sooner or later. I was hoping that you would not give him to me."

"He is too rough for you," the Earl answered her firmly.

"I am quite content to agree with that," Melva said. "And you do realise that you cannot go away and leave me alone with him."

They rode on a little way in silence and then Melva asked,

"When are you expecting your wife?"

The Earl had almost forgotten that he had said he had one and so it took him a few seconds to recollect his thoughts before he replied,

"I don't know. She cannot leave the old relative she is with at the moment."

"I am glad about that," Melva told him. "I have a feeling that when she arrives you will want to leave us."

"Why do you say that?" the Earl enquired.

"Because you were telling Papa last night that you thought I should have more friends and if possible spend a Season in London."

"I thought that you had gone up to bed," the Earl muttered.

"I heard you mention my name so I waited to hear what you were saying," Melva confessed.

"Would you like a Season in London?" the Earl enquired.

There was silence for a moment and then, as they rode on, Melva responded,

"I am not sure. It is something I have never done and I think that I would be rather intimidated by meeting so many people I have never met before."

"You will be a huge success," the Earl said firmly. "You are very pretty and I gather from your father that he can afford to pay a distinguished chaperone who would get you invited to all the best dances and the most interesting parties."

They rode on for several minutes before Melva said,

"Do you think that I would really enjoy it? It is something I have never done and I think I should feel like a fish out of water."

"I think that you will take London by storm," the Earl said, "and receive at least half-a-dozen proposals the first month you are there."

"Proposals?"

"I mean proposals of marriage," the Earl explained. "Every *debutante* knows if she is a success or not from the amount of men who propose to her. I am ready to predict that there will be quite a large number. You will be able to pick and choose who you want as a husband."

"Why should they want to marry me?" she asked.

The Earl thought that this was a question he had not been asked before.

"Because you are so lovely to look at and because your father is a distinguished man and, as you are his heir, you will have some money of your own eventually."

He realised that Melva was thinking it over.

They had ridden for quite a long way before Melva said,

"That is not what I want."

The Earl looked at her in surprise.

"What do you want?" he asked.

"I think really that I want to see a little of the world before I worry about marriage," Melva replied. "And I would never marry anyone however important or however rich he was unless I loved him. Mama and Papa fell in love the moment they first met. I expect you realise that Papa was much older than her."

"I thought perhaps that was so, because you are so young."

"Mama told me," Melva said, "the moment she saw Papa that she thought that he was the most exciting man she could ever imagine. He told her a little later that he knew the moment he saw her that he had been looking for her all his life."

"So they were married and you were born and what happened to your mother?"

"She was never very strong," Melva replied, "and three years ago when I was fifteen – she had a heart attack. No one quite knows why – but she never recovered from it."

There was a sob in Melva's voice and the Earl said,

"I am sorry, very sorry."

"It was terrible for Papa. He loved her so much. Although I have tried to make up for her loss, he misses her – every moment and so it is – difficult to talk to him about her."

The Earl did not quite know what to say.

They rode on in silence.

Then, as if Melva had been thinking it all over, she quizzed him,

"When you fell in love, what did you feel?"

The Earl hesitated and then he answered her,

"I think what everyone feels when they are really in love is that they want to spend the rest of their life with that particular person and nothing else in the whole world is of any consequence."

"That is what I thought," Melva said, "and that is what I hope I will feel."

She hesitated for a moment before she persisted,

"Did you know the moment you saw your wife that she was the one person in the world you wanted?"

The Earl wished that he did not have to lie about his mythical wife.

Yet he thought maybe that, because she was talking about it, what he was saying now would help Melva in the future.

"I think," he said, "that for some people it is love at first sight. For others they take a little time to realise how significant that particular person is to them."

"And then?"

The Earl smiled,

"Then, of course, they live happily ever after."

Melva gave a little murmur.

"That is what I want. I always love the end of a Fairy story."

The Earl mused that a great number of people were still trying to make the Fairy story of their youth come true.

He supposed if he was honest that is exactly what he wanted as well, but he thought it very unlikely that he would ever find it.

To change the subject he suggested,

"These horses are being lazy. I will race you to the end of the field.

Melva did not argue and she pushed Dragonfly into a spirited gallop.

She rode so well that the Earl was nearly defeated.

It was only by a superb piece of horsemanship that he managed to edge ahead of her. And that was just before they were obliged to come to a standstill.

Melva's pretty cheeks were flushed and her eyes were shining.

"You are too good," she admitted, "and I did so want to beat you, Mr. Stanford."

"So why should you want to?" the Earl asked. "A woman should always want a man to be victorious whether it is in riding or any other field."

"I suppose you will say that he has to be victorious in love too," Melva smiled.

"But, of course," the Earl agreed. "It is a battle for survival and the man must obviously be the victor."

He thought as he was speaking that that was what he had managed to be.

He had eluded the designs of his father, the Queen and Princess Gilberta and he silently congratulated himself on having done so.

Then he heard Melva say very quietly as if she was speaking to herself,

"That is just how I like a man – to be victorious."

The Earl gazed at her.

He now wondered as he had wondered before what would happen to her and, if she just stayed here and saw no one, it would be a tragedy.

She was now gently smoothing her long fair hair back from her forehead.

As it caught the sunshine, it seemed to sparkle and her face, as she turned towards him, was incredibly lovely.

Their eyes met and then for some seconds neither of them could look away.

Then the Earl said almost harshly,

"Now we will go back. I want to take those jumps again and we have to decide which horses we are going to ride this afternoon."

He turned his horse as he spoke.

He then started to ride quickly back the way they had come without waiting for Melva.

He told himself as he did so that Nanny must have good news for him soon or else he would undoubtedly be wise to explore a little more of Cornwall.

Then he could start wending his way slowly back towards Shelbourne Towers and Oxfordshire.

He could take a different route to the way he had come and that in itself would definitely be entertaining.

'If I stay here too long,' he argued, 'I shall become involved with these people I am staying with. That would be a mistake. I am just a ship passing in the night and once I am gone they will find someone to take my place and forget me.'

He was then aware that Melva was approaching him.

Quite suddenly he wanted to run away.

He whipped up his horse.

As he already had several lengths start, he was back in the paddock some way ahead of her.

She galloped in.

Then, without checking the speed of Dragonfly, she took him straight to the highest jump.

The Earl parted his lips to stop her.

They had ridden quite a long way and it would be a mistake to try the jumps again without warning.

But he was too late.

Melva put Dragonfly at the jump and he rose to the challenge splendidly.

He did not, however, land as well as he had before.

As he staggered on impact, Melva fell forward in her saddle.

For a moment the Earl thought that she would fall over the horse's head.

He then gave a shout of terror.

But by sheer luck she managed to save herself.

Dragonfly did not fall and, as he dragged himself to his feet, Melva remained in the saddle.

It all happened so quickly.

Yet, as the Earl knew only too well, it might have been disastrous.

He had held his breath.

Now, as he could start breathing again, he realised just how much the near-miss incident had perturbed him.

How frightened he had been that Melva might fall and injure herself.

As he now rode forward to go to her side, he was suddenly aware how much it mattered to him.

Pulling in the reins, he then brought Dragonfly to a standstill and, as he reached Melva, he asked,

"Are you alright?"

His voice sounded strange even to himself.

Melva turned to look at him and he saw that for the moment she was a little shaken.

"I am all – right," she said in a hesitating voice. "I knew – I was wrong in taking the fence without waiting for you – to tell me to do so."

She spoke just like a child who was frightened that it would be punished for being naughty.

Without meaning to do so, the Earl put out his hand and laid it on hers.

He realised that she was trembling and he said,

"It does not matter. Nothing matters as long as you are not hurt."

Only as she smiled did he realise how much she meant to him.

They went back to the house and found the General waiting for luncheon.

"You are late," he pointed out as they came into the dining room.

"I am very sorry, Papa," Melva said, "but we went further than we expected. The horses jumped very well and you would have been proud of them."

"Tell me about it in the dining room," the General insisted. "Hurry up and wash. I am hungry."

"I am sure that means you have finished a chapter of your book," Melva remarked as she ran up the stairs.

"How did the horses fare?" the General asked the Earl.

"They took the jump which I raised six inches last night without any difficulty, but your daughter nearly had a fall on our way back and I think she is a little shaken."

"For Heaven's sake don't let her do too much," the General said. "She is incredibly brave. At the same time horses can be unpredictable and I have always been afraid, as she is so small, she might hurt herself."

"I will be very careful, General," the Earl replied.

He went to wash his face and hands and brush back his hair.

Then he joined the General who had already gone into the dining room.

They usually had a light luncheon, but an extremely well-planned meal at dinner.

"I intended to go riding this afternoon," the General said, as the Earl joined them, "but I have reached a very critical part of my book, so I think that you will have to ride without me."

He had just finished speaking when Melva came in.

"I am sorry, Papa," she said. "It's my fault that we are late."

"I was only just saying," the General replied, "that I shall not go riding this afternoon and, if you have had a bit of trouble this morning, I should do something else."

"That is a good idea," the Earl agreed. "What I would like to do, if at all possible, is to look at some of the smugglers' caves which I am told are very interesting."

"Yes, of course, we can do that," Melva piped up.

"I want to drive my horses," the Earl said, "because they are feeling rather neglected."

Melva laughed.

"It was what Dragonfly was feeling this morning, so, of course, we must take your beautiful white horses for a drive."

"There are plenty of smugglers' caves here for you to see," the General commented. "As you will surely know smuggling has been going on here since the twelfth century and, I believe, is still happening more frequently than we think."

"A great deal of what we hear," the Earl suggested, "is, I am sure, just a Fairytale. People like to think that smuggling is as bad on the South coast as it was during the Napoleonic War, but actually there is now very little taking place and, what there is, is of no great threat."

"I would agree with you," the General said, "and, of course, smugglers were most dangerous when they were supplying Napoleon with the money to buy arms that he could then use against us."

"They also carried spies into Britain," the Earl said, "which I always thought was unforgivable. With such a long length of coastline it was impossible for the Riding Officers or anyone else to keep them away."

The General chuckled.

"I have always been sorry for the Riding Officer. Here in Cornwall he was allotted four miles of coast and he had to provide himself with a horse."

"Was he well paid?" the Earl enquired.

"I think very little and he certainly earned what he received. He was on patrol both day and night visiting the places most likely for a run."

The General paused before he went on,

"The Riding Officers here were told to always be properly armed and to keep their movements as secret as possible."

"He had to work too," Melva chimed in, "with the Dragoons who were stationed with Riding Officers and, of course, with the off-sea Cruisers."

"It sounds an impossible task," the Earl exclaimed. "I am only surprised that they found enough men to take on the job."

"It was a very dangerous job because the man was alone," the General said. "But I have already found that where a job is dangerous there are always volunteers who feel it is a challenge they cannot refuse."

The Earl nodded.

"I think that is true. The moment one asks in the Army for men to take on a special mission one gets more results than one needs."

The General smiled.

"That is indeed true and I like to think it is only the English who are so brave."

"I will tell you one thing about the smugglers here," Melva said to the Earl. "The Commissioner had to make it a strict rule that every man who collected the prize money must have actually been present when the seizure of the smugglers was made. Otherwise those who sat at home managed to obtain as much as those who had seized the smugglers and the contraband they were handling."

The Earl laughed.

"I can see that happening here just as it must have happened a thousand times along the South coast. There is no doubt that during the War some people made a fortune."

"I have read that the smugglers took home French prisoners of war," Melva said.

"The most notorious of all West Country smugglers was Jack Rattenbury," the General said, "who was caught after he agreed to take four French Officers back to France for one hundred and fifty pounds. They were all arrested, but apparently Rattenbury was clever enough to persuade the Court that he was taking the Frenchmen to Jersey."

"And he got away with it?" the Earl enquired.

"Yes, the Magistrates dismissed him."

"He was indeed lucky. At the same time I always understood that the smugglers took risks that no one else would have dared to."

"Whatever they did then or did not do," the General said, "they were a nuisance. I am always hoping that we have heard the last of them in Cornwall."

"There certainly cannot be as many as there used to be," Melva said. "So I will take Mr. Stanford to look at the different caves where they used to hide their spoils. Who knows, perhaps we will find a long forgotten barrel of vintage brandy!"

The General grinned.

"I think that is unlikely. But if you have good luck we will drink it this evening."

"That is a promise," Melva said.

They rose from the table.

The Earl went to fetch his chaise and the two white horses.

Melva ran upstairs to her bedroom to take off her riding skirt and blouse.

She put on a very pretty cotton dress, which made her look like the flowers in the fields outside.

As she tidied her hair, she thought how exciting it was that there was someone to do things with her.

Otherwise she would have had to sit at home alone while her father wrote yet another chapter of his book.

'Mr. Stanford is so handsome,' she told herself. 'I cannot think how his wife can leave him for so long. She must want so much to be with him and he too must find it very frustrating.'

At the same time she hoped he enjoyed being here with her father and her at The Manor House.

He certainly seemed happy with the horses and she knew that he liked talking with her father.

They talked about the difficulties and privations of war and the political situation in Europe, which Melva found absorbing as well.

She longed to visit France and she would like above everything else to see the beautiful Churches in Italy and the statues of the Gods and Goddesses in Greece.

Because the General had no son, she had in many ways had a boy's education. It had been easier when she was growing up to have Tutors from Penzance rather than Governesses.

When Mr. Stanford talked about India, she thought how lucky he had been to have visited that exotic country.

How wonderful it would be if she could travel abroad when she was older and, as she was so practical, she told herself firmly that it all really rested on whom she married.

It might be to a man who wanted to stay at home and then she would see no more of the world than she had seen at the moment.

If, however, he was adventurous then perhaps she would not only see Europe but North Africa and these were the places that her father had visited as a soldier.

It was stimulating at any rate now to talk about the smugglers.

Mr. Stanford must be told about the ruthless way they had managed to board French and Spanish ships and then carry away their loot.

'I am sure that he too will have a lot to tell me about them,' she thought as she went downstairs.

The front door was open and she saw that the white horses were waiting for her.

Mr. Stanford was in the driving seat with one of the stable boys in the back seat behind the hood.

She ran down the steps and climbed in beside the Earl.

"This is so exciting!" she enthused, as he started his horses off. "Let's pretend we are smugglers and see what we can find to bring back for Papa this afternoon!"

The Earl smiled.

"I cannot imagine that you look like a smuggler. I have always imagined them as grim, ugly and rather dirty men, but then you look as if you had just stepped out of a bandbox!"

Melva gave a little laugh.

"This is a compliment and the first one you have paid me. Others have always been to the horse I am riding, but not for me."

The Earl thought that any other woman would have complained long ago and he would have felt remiss in not telling her that she was lovely.

However, he was not only playing the part of the man who looked after the horses.

He did not wish to spoil anything that was perfect and Melva had no idea of her own attractions.

She did not expect him to answer what she had just said.

She was already talking of the way they should go and how close they would be able to get to the smugglers' caves.

"I hope you have good shoes," she said, "because we shall have to leave the horses and walk quite a way."

"I still have the use of my legs," the Earl answered.

"I am aware of that," Melva said, "but you must admit that if you have a horse to ride it is quite unnecessary to walk."

"I agree with that and, you are right, a long walk on flat feet will doubtless do us a great deal of good."

"My feet are not flat," Melva protested indignantly.

Then they were both laughing.

CHAPTER FIVE

They drove for quite some way with Melva giving instructions.

The Earl thought nothing could be more beautiful than the rolling countryside they were passing through.

Occasionally he could see the remains of a castle or a few cottages clustered together.

Otherwise it seemed like an empty world with only Melva and his horses in it.

When they had driven for about two miles, Melva told him to stop.

It was a convenient place where there were trees to give shelter to the horses.

They were on a road that seemed to go nowhere, winding between the brilliant flowering fields.

"Now we will have to walk," Melva said, "and I am longing to see how good you are at it."

"I expect that I shall do better than you," the Earl replied. "Actually when I am at home I walk a great deal."

He was thinking of the long days shooting on the Shelbourne Estate, also when he was grouse shooting in the North of Scotland.

After the moors he climbed every year, he did not think he would find the Cornish land that difficult.

He had, however, been very careful since he arrived not to say anything about his home and the few questions that Melva did ask him he had answered her briefly and somewhat evasively.

Because she was very perceptive he thought that she was aware that he did not want to talk about himself or his wife and he much admired her tact in not pursuing the subject.

As she stepped down now, he saw that she had flat sandshoes on her feet and wished that he had thought of wearing his tennis shoes.

He handed over the reins to Albert the groom he had brought with them.

"Now stay here, Albert," he said, "and don't worry if we take a long time. You will find the horses no trouble, but if they become restless, take them for a short drive and then come back again."

"I'll do that, Mr. Stanford," Albert replied.

He was the most intelligent of the young grooms and that was why the Earl had brought him along with them today.

He patted the horses and urged,

"Do look after them, Albert, because they are very precious to me."

"I knows that," Albert answered, "and I'll take care nobody steals 'em."

It then struck the Earl that the highwayman was still at large.

And he went back to the seat he had been driving on and felt down for the revolver.

He pulled it from its usual place and said to Albert,

"This is loaded and I want you to carry it carefully in your pocket. If by any chance someone tries to steal the horses, shoot him in the arm or the leg, but not the body. Do you understand?"

He saw that Albert was listening with an expectant look in his eyes.

"If a man with a mask approaches anywhere near you, fire a bullet into the air. Tell him, as I did the other day, that the next bullet will be in his body. Unless he is very persistent, you will find that he will run away."

"I'll do just what you tells me," Albert answered.

He had taken the revolver from the Earl and was holding it in his hands as if it was the most exciting object he had ever touched.

"Now be very careful," the Earl went on, "and do not fire it by mistake. Remember you can kill a person or an animal very easily."

"I'll be real careful, Mr. Stanford. I've 'andled a gun afore, but I've never seen such a small one as this."

The Earl thought it was unlikely that the very latest style of revolver had yet reached as far as Cornwall.

Melva was waiting a little way ahead of him and he therefore said,

"Now remember what I have said to you, Albert."

"I will," he promised.

The Earl hurried to join Melva.

He saw that there was a winding path through the field where she was standing.

It rose higher and higher and in the far distance the flowers appeared to be touching the sky.

They set off at a sharp pace and, when they reached the top of the field, the Earl could see the sea far below them and there was a gorge surrounded by rugged cliffs.

As they began to climb down, he could see the dark surface of the rocks.

There were gulls perched on the ledges of the cliffs, but there was no sign of any human habitation.

If they avoided the rocks, the Earl could appreciate that this deep gorge was the perfect place for smugglers to hide their wares.

And then beyond the gorge there was the turbulent Atlantic Ocean and even though the day was warm and calm the waves with their white foam crashed against the rocks with great force.

He could imagine only too well how rough they would be in a flood tide.

Melva knew her way.

She walked without hesitation over slippery rocks to show the Earl a cavern in the cliffs.

They jumped from rock to rock to reach it.

When finally they did so, the Earl saw that it was a perfect place for smugglers.

They could leave their loot here until they could take it out to sea in a ship, which would be bigger or faster than the one they had brought it in here immediately after its capture.

The Earl knew the difficulties a smuggler might face in getting rid of what he had stolen.

Yet, if they had looted wine from a French ship, there would always be a large number of people eagerly waiting to receive it.

The Squire liked his brandy and so did his Lady, who gave smart parties and even the Vicar of a Parish participated in his own fashion.

Luggers with a thousand yards of canvas in their mainsail could cross the Channel in eight hours.

And a cargo bought for one thousand five hundred pounds in France could be easily sold in England for three thousand pounds, ensuring a handsome profit.

Where there was not a place in the cliffs where a large cargo could be delivered safely, it was carried across country at night in wagons drawn by horses with muffled hooves.

It was impossible not to feel that smuggling was romantic and exciting and the Earl knew that was how Melva found it.

They inspected the first cavern and Melva looked carefully for a trace of anything that had been smuggled, but she was disappointed.

"I am afraid that your father will have to go without his brandy for dinner tonight," the Earl joked as they went back into the sunshine.

"I have two more caverns to show you," Melva said, "and they are better than any of the others along the coast."

The Earl was quite prepared to follow her, but he found the slippery wet stones rather dangerous and he had no wish to fall into the seawater.

Melva moved ahead of him springing from rock to rock effortlessly like a nymph.

She had a grace that he could not help admiring.

Under the tall cliffs soaring up towards the sky she looked like a Fairy or a flower blown by the wind.

Finally she leapt from a rock onto the side of the cliffs where there was a large break in the wall.

The Earl followed her a little gingerly and he was glad when his feet were on firmer ground.

This cavern was much larger than the first one they had seen and its floor was sandy.

It had a high ceiling overhead and light was coming through the broken cliff sides.

"You can imagine how much loot this would hold," Melva suggested.

Her voice seemed to echo.

"I certainly think it would be safe here," the Earl agreed. "It would be too difficult for the Riding Officer to poke in his nose to see what he could find."

Melva laughed.

"He certainly could not do so on his horse. And look over here, I think there is another cavern connected with this one."

She moved towards the end of the one where they were standing.

"Personally," the Earl said, "I think I have seen enough. We might as well go back."

"Oh, I have another cave to show you yet," Melva cried. "I will just have a look at this one."

She walked quickly away from him.

The Earl went back towards the opening through which they had just entered the cavern.

As he reached it, he heard her scream and turned round.

"What is it?" he called out.

Melva screamed again.

Now he started to run towards the end of the cavern which was in darkness.

It flashed through his mind that she had fallen into the sea or perhaps down some hole in the rocky ground.

He reached the opening she had passed through.

Before he could realise what was happening he was seized by three men.

He started to struggle.

As he did so, a gag was pulled over his mouth and tied at the back of his head.

He fought as violently as he could but was helpless.

There were two men holding him captive and a third man joining in as soon as he was gagged.

It was difficult to see them, as there was much less light where he was now than there had been in the outer cavern.

The Earl could now gradually make out that his assailants were large men with caps pulled down over their heads.

Their rough clothes made him sure that they were smugglers.

They were winding a rope tightly round him so that it hurt his arms and his legs.

Because it had been so warm, he had taken off his coat before they had left the horses and had started to climb the hill and he was only wearing his shirt and trousers.

With a speed that quite obviously came from long practice, the men tied the rope round him.

Then they flung him down roughly onto the floor of the cavern.

His back was against the side of the cavern and his head was bruised by the hard stones he had fallen on.

It was only then he became aware that Melva was already in the same position on the ground.

She too was gagged and her feet were tied together by her ankles while her arms were behind her back.

The Earl could only just see her.

Now, when he was no longer being pushed around, he looked at the men who had tied him up.

There were five of them and he then realised that two of them must have been dealing with Melva and the other three had concentrated on him.

They were now looking down at their prisoners.

The Earl could not see their faces clearly and yet he was certain that they were thinking how helpless he and Melva now were.

Then one man spoke and he had a broad Cornish accent,

"What shall we do with 'em?" he asked in a low voice.

"Shall we push 'em in the sea?" another man said.

They were asking a man who was a little taller than the rest.

"Floating bodies," he replied, "will attract attention. We'll pick 'em up tonight when we comes back wiv the ship."

The men nodded their heads as if that made sense.

But to the Earl it was a death knell.

He knew what happened to prisoners on smuggling ships.

A man was dropped overboard far out at sea and it was difficult to identify him by the time the waves swept him ashore several days later.

The Earl wondered frantically what he could do.

For the moment he could only listen to the men standing in the middle of the cavern.

It was very much smaller than the one that he and Melva had entered at first and, when he looked behind the men, he realised why it was so small.

It was filled with barrels and wooden boxes and he was quite sure that the boxes contained bottles of wine or brandy.

The man who had last spoken turned towards the entrance, which was narrow and only large enough to let one man move through it carefully.

It passed through the Earl's mind that the barrels must have come through the larger cavern.

"Let's go and get the ship," one of the smugglers suggested.

"Suppose someone's lookin' for these people?" one of the other men asked.

"Then they just won't find 'em," was the answer. "Two tourists ain't of no importance."

As the smuggler said the last word, he then slipped through the opening.

With only a backward glance the others followed him one by one.

The Earl listened.

He heard them, he thought, moving over the rocks, but then the continual crashing of the rough sea made it impossible to be certain of anything.

As the last smuggler disappeared from his view, he looked towards Melva.

He wondered what on earth they could do.

She was as incapable as he was.

It meant that when the smugglers returned, as they intended, they would load up their ship.

And he and Melva would be taken aboard.

There was no need to even ask himself what would happen next as he knew the answer only too well.

Whether they were killed before they even left the cavern or when they were pushed into the sea, the result would be the same.

He and Melva would die ignominiously.

And no one would ever find out exactly what had happened to them.

'How in God's name,' the Earl asked himself, 'am I going to get out of this?'

It was then to his astonishment that he heard Melva speak and her voice was only a little louder than a whisper.

"Are you all right?"

He turned his head with some difficulty.

He could see her propped up against the stone wall beside him.

To his surprise the gag had fallen from her mouth.

His gag had been put on in a most professional manner through his teeth.

Almost as if he had asked the question, Melva said,

"I had a Nanny once – who, if I told a lie, always made me wear a gag for at least an hour. I managed by twisting my head as she put it on to hold a little between my teeth so that I could loosen it when she thought that it would be impossible for me to speak."

The Earl had never thought of this before and only wished that he could do it himself.

"What I have to do now," Melva said, "is to undo your gag. Can you somehow move nearer to me and turn your head away so that I can reach it?"

The Earl wanted to tell her how clever he thought she was being, but it was impossible for him to speak and very difficult for him to move.

He managed, however, with a tremendous effort to push himself a little nearer to Melva.

At the same time she endeavoured to reach him.

Then he turned his head and eased himself down a little lower.

Now her lips were opposite the knot in the gag at the back of his neck.

It took time.

Actually it seemed longer than it was for Melva to bite away at the coarse cloth that the Earl had been gagged with.

Fortunately the smugglers had not knotted it very tightly as they obviously thought it would be impossible for him to remove it.

Finally it fell loose and, as the Earl wriggled his lips out of it, he exclaimed,

"That was very clever of you! Thank you, Melva. Now we have to get out of this ghastly position we are in before they come back."

"I heard what they said," Melva said in a low voice. "And I am frightened, very frightened."

It was the first time that she had admitted it.

But the Earl had known when her body was against his back that she was trembling.

Deliberately making his voice sound quite normal and unperturbed, he said quietly,

"Now what I have to do is to release your hands. You have freed my teeth and now it is my turn to put them to work!"

Malva gave a little sob.

"Suppose – you cannot manage it?"

"I can manage anything," the Earl said firmly, "and I intend to save you and me from those unpleasant devils. Thank God it will be a long time before they come back."

He thought as he spoke that it was a good thing that they had left the General earlier as he was in a hurry to go back and write his book.

And so there was still most of the afternoon ahead of them.

"Now get as near to me as you can," the Earl said, "and turn away so that I can reach your hands."

He pushed himself forward until he was lying on the floor.

His face was then level with Melva's hands which were tied behind her.

The smugglers had wound the rope first round her body, then round her wrists and they had knotted the ends of the rope together.

Fortunately there was only one knot and they had clearly thought it impossible for her to move with so much rope around her.

Her feet were tied together with a separate rope and the Earl began to work with his teeth, finding the taste of the coarse rope most unpleasant.

At the same time it was old and it must have been brought to the cave with the loot which was piled on the wall opposite them.

The rope could, he thought, have joined two barrels that a man could then carry suspended from his shoulders or alternatively it could have merely knotted two of the boxes together.

Whatever else it was, the rope was very tough and dirty.

He had had to spit several times to prevent himself from swallowing pieces of it.

Finally, after what had seemed to be a very long time, although actually it was not much more than a quarter of an hour, Melva's hands were free.

She shook them to bring back the circulation.

Then, pulling the long rope down over her body, she unfastened the one that held her ankles together.

The Earl was lying on his back watching her.

Then, as she threw the rope to one side, she said,

"Now I must do the same to you."

"I have a better idea," the Earl replied, "and I can assure you this rope does not make a particularly pleasant meal!"

"I am sure it was horrible," Melva agreed, "but I must set you free."

"Now you will have to be clever about it," the Earl said. "Go and look amongst those boxes and barrels for any sort of implement. A knife would be a Godsend, but I doubt if you will find one."

Malva rose to her feet.

She smoothed down her dress as if to sweep away the feeling of horror she had when the smugglers had tied her up.

She was still feeling desperately afraid.

However, she forced herself to think not about what had happened but how she could free Mr. Stanford.

There were not many places she could look for an implement, as the barrels were piled closely against the wall of the cavern with the boxes on top of them.

When she looked into the boxes, she saw that each one contained twelve bottles.

She thought it must be brandy and she remembered that she had said jokingly that they would take a bottle back for her father.

"There is nothing here except bottles," she said aloud, "and I think it's brandy."

"Take a bottle out of the box," the Earl said.

Melva managed this with a little difficulty as the bottles were tied into place.

Finally she managed to pull one out and then turned round with it in her hands.

"Here it is," she said.

"Good!" the Earl replied. "Now this is what I want you to do. First try and pull out the cork, but, if that is impossible, we will achieve what we want another way."

Melva did not understand what he was trying to do.

But, as she was terrified of not being able to escape, it was easier to obey him than to ask questions.

She tried very hard with her fingers, but the neck of the cork was deep into the bottle and it was impossible to free it.

"I cannot do it," she admitted finally.

"Then come over here," the Earl said, "and stand beside me."

She did as she was told wondering what he was intending to do.

"Now," he said, "throw the bottle of brandy as hard as you can and with all your strength against that wall. I want it to break."

Melva still did not understand.

Yet, because he was so positive, she just had to obey him.

Holding the bottle in two hands over her head, she drew in her breath.

Then she threw it as hard as she could against the wall.

There was a crash and the bottle broke and fell to the ground. There was now a strong smell of spirit in the cavern.

"Good!" the Earl exclaimed. "Now what we want is a small stone but it must be flat."

Melva then went to the opening of the cavern and spied round the corner half-afraid that the smugglers might be watching her.

Right at the foot of the cavern she saw between the cliff and a rock that there were piles of pebbles.

The tide was out otherwise she was quite certain that she would not have been able to see them.

She then bent down and, after turning over the wet pebbles for some moments, she found a flat stone.

It was a little larger than a two shilling piece and she picked it up and went back to the Earl.

"Will this do?" she asked.

"Excellent!" he cried. "Now put it under the rope which covers my hands, then pick up the sharpest piece of glass. I can see there is a piece there which belongs to the top of the bottle."

Melva turned round to look for it.

"It will take time," the Earl went on. "But, if you work it as hard as you can, it should cut the rope and that is more effective than spoiling your teeth."

"You are brilliant!" Melva said. "I would never have thought of anything like that and my teeth are indeed very precious!"

"You would look very strange without them," the Earl remarked and she had to laugh.

It seemed to her to take a very long time to cut the rope against the flat stone.

Finally she did it and he shook his wrists free.

He then bent forward to untie the rope round his legs. It broke his nails and once or twice he swore beneath his breath.

Yet finally the Earl's feet were free and he then stood up holding his arms above his head.

Melva had been watching him and she had prayed all the time she had worked on the rope round his hands.

Now she gave a cry of delight,

"We are free! We are free!"

Without thinking she flung herself against the Earl.

He brought down his arms from above his head and put them round her.

Just for a moment he hugged her.

Then without even meaning to his lips found hers.

He kissed her and they were both very still.

With an effort the Earl said,

"Come, let's get out of here."

His voice sounded strange even to himself.

Without glancing at Melva, he walked through the opening into the larger cavern.

He hurried towards the far end of it and she had to run to keep up with him.

By the time she caught up with him he was already walking back over the slippery rocks.

She had led him before, but now he was leading her.

Only as they both reached the dip in the cliffs down which they had come did he put out his hand to pull her up beside him.

Then they were back in the flower-filled field and they could see the twisting lane below them.

Beneath the trees there were the two white horses and Albert waiting for them.

"We have done it! We have done it!" Melva cried.

Now there was a tremor in her voice and she was speaking more softly.

"We have been incredibly lucky," the Earl said. "Now I am going to take you home to safety. It is the last time we will ever go looking for smugglers."

"How could we have known? How could we have guessed," Melva asked, "that they were there? If I had not been so stupid as to go into the further cavern, we should never even have known about them."

The Earl realised there was still a note of fear in her voice.

Her fingers, which he was holding, were trembling.

"Forget it!" he said quickly. "It is over now. You are safe and no one will hurt you."

"I thought when they said they would take us out to sea we would drown and never be heard of again," Melva whispered.

"We have been fortunate enough to have defeated them and that is all that matters," the Earl sighed.

They walked down the path for a while before he added,

"I think it would be wise to say nothing of what has happened. If your father informs the Chief Constable, they will most certainly be able to confiscate the brandy before the smugglers take it away."

He paused before continuing,

"They might be able to apprehend the smugglers themselves. But that means Police proceedings and you and I would have to give evidence."

"No! No!" Melva exclaimed. "I don't want to think of it. I am sure that it was my prayers that saved us or perhaps, as you thought of everything, it was one of King Arthur's Knights who told you what to do."

The Earl smiled.

"I had forgotten that King Arthur hunted in this County," he said. "Of course Tintagel was his birthplace."

"He was a Cornish King," she said proudly, "and I often think of him. Now because you saved us so bravely perhaps in another life you were one of his Knights."

"I am delighted to think so," the Earl replied. "But we must remember that, if you had not been clever enough to be able to talk to me, it might have been very different."

"I am quite certain that it was King Arthur who helped us," Melva said, "and, you are right, we will not tell even Papa what occurred. I am sure he would want to take away all that brandy before the smugglers do and he could only do that if we reported it in great detail to the Chief Constable."

"Then it will be a secret just between us," the Earl confirmed.

He turned to look at Melva as he spoke.

As their eyes met, he felt a very strange feeling in the region of his body that he thought of as his heart.

He could still feel the softness and sweetness of her lips and it had seemed to him as he kissed her that she was different to any other woman he had ever kissed.

Quickly he looked ahead and hurried towards the horses.

'I am falling in love,' he said to himself, 'so the sooner I leave here the better.'

He continued to think,

'Having just escaped from marriage to a German Princess, I could not be so silly as to be caught by a pretty Cornish girl.'

"You are going too fast," Melva said. "The horses are quite safe. I can see them and they have not run away."

"Nor has anyone tried to steal them," he managed to say.

Melva was still clinging to his hand and he had not taken it away.

Now, as they reached the road, he set her free and walked towards the chaise.

"Have the horses been all right, Albert?" he asked.

The groom smiled.

"They be as good as gold, Mr. Stanford. Did you find anythin' interestin'?"

"Nothing we could bring back with us," the Earl replied.

He climbed into the chaise and picked up the reins.

Melva joined him and Albert jumped up behind.

Despite his efforts not to, the Earl found himself gazing at Melva.

She was, he thought, a little pale.

Her eyes, because she was no longer frightened, seemed larger than they had before.

She was still unmistakeably lovely.

Then, as he looked at her lips, he felt again that strange feeling within his breast.

It was something he had felt once or twice before, but not in the same way that he was feeling it now.

He told himself it was just an attraction for a pretty woman, one who had behaved remarkably bravely in the most unexpected and outrageous situation.

Equally his brain told him that it was much more than that.

It was something that he had never known in his life before.

Yet in the back of his mind he had sought for it, but was almost certain that it did not exist.

It was something so different, in fact so wonderful that it was what men had sought throughout the ages as they had searched for the Holy Grail.

Deliberately the Earl cracked his whip and drove his horses quicker than he usually did.

'What I am feeling is not real,' he told himself. 'It is just Cornwall, all this talk of King Arthur, his Knights and the myths and legends that have no foundation. In fact I must get back to reality as quickly as I can.'

As he drove on with his eyes on the road, he was vividly conscious of Melva sitting quietly beside him.

It took them half the time to reach the General's house than it had to drive away from it.

As they sped down the drive, the horses seemed to be in the same hurry as their driver.

As they clattered into the courtyard, the Earl and Melva saw to their surprise that there were a number of carriages parked there.

Some were closed, some were open like the chaise and one was definitely an aged phaeton driven by three horses.

"Who can be here?" Melva asked. "Who are all these people?"

The Earl did not answer.

She jumped out almost before the horses had come to a standstill and the Earl deliberately did not hurry to follow her.

He handed the reins to Albert and told him to take the horses straight to the stables.

He then gave him special instructions as to how to groom them. It was what Albert had heard already several times, but he listened attentively.

"I'll do what you says, Mr. Stanford," he said as the Earl paused for breath.

When the Earl turned towards the front door, he saw that Melva had disappeared.

He wondered what was happening and he felt that it was only polite to inform the General that they had now returned.

He heard voices in the drawing room and walked in.

To his surprise it seemed to be filled with people.

There were quite a number of good-looking young men and two young women who might have been the same age as Melva.

There was a tall elderly man talking to the General.

"Oh, here you are," the General said, as the Earl came in. "I have just been relating to my brother what a success you have been with my horses over the last few months."

The man beside the General held out his hand.

"I congratulate you," he said. "I have never known my brother find anyone who treated his horses exactly as he wanted."

The General laughed and then he said,

"That is not fair. I must admit I have had one fool after another, but Stanford, as I have already told you, is entirely different. You will be able to see for yourself."

"I am looking forward to that," the man said. "By the way, as we have not yet been introduced. My name is Sir Wilfred Wymond. I have just told my brother that I have bought Tintagel Castle, which is only a short distance from here."

"I had no idea that was what he was thinking of doing," the General said. "But, of course, it is delightful for me and it will be wonderful for Melva to have friends and relatives of her own age nearby."

"There are certainly enough of them," Sir Wilfred remarked.

As if he thought the Earl needed an explanation, he added,

"I have four sons and two daughters and all of them seldom move anywhere without a crowd of young friends of their own age. Melva will no longer be lonely as I feel she is at the moment."

The Earl looked across the big room.

Now he could see Melva surrounded by a gaggle of young men and it was just as he had told her she would be if she went to London.

In a way London had come to her and he could see how eagerly the men were talking to her.

She looked very pretty in the midst of them.

He felt as he looked at her again that unmistakeable feeling in his heart.

Now it was even more intense than it had been before.

Sir Wilfred left his brother's side and joined those who were talking to Melva.

The General turned to the Earl.

"I have had the surprise of my life," he said. "I had no idea my brother was interested in Tintagel Castle which, as you are aware, is connected in everyone's mind with King Arthur. It will need a great deal done to it, of course, but my brother is a rich man."

He thought the Earl was looking interested and he added,

"Perhaps I should explain. He is the sixth Baronet and is the Head of the Wymond family. I received my Knighthood from Queen Victoria soon after I was made a General."

The Earl realised that it was for his success in the battlefield.

The General chuckled.

"It is unusual to have two titles in the same family, I would readily admit, but then the Wymonds have always been rather different from anyone else. That will certainly be said of them now when they are moving into Tintagel Castle!"

He paused for a moment before he went on,

"My brother has already asked me to help him with the horses he will require and with four sons and all their friends that will be quite a large amount. That, Stanford, is where you will come in. I shall need your help in buying what is required, although, of course, they can borrow our horses for the time being."

The General did not wait for the Earl to reply.

As if he found his brother and his nephews and nieces irresistible, he then turned towards the crowd that surrounded Melva.

The Earl watched him go and then he walked out of the room and made his way to the stables.

CHAPTER SIX

Sir Wilfred Wymond turned to his brother,

"I hope, Aubin, you will be kind enough to give us dinner? As we have just arrived at The Castle, I very much doubt if there will be anything to eat in the place."

"Of course you can stay for dinner," the General replied. "I am sure that there will be enough to go round, even though it might be rather a mixed meal."

He sent Melva to tell the cook what was happening and then she hurried back to join her cousins.

They were telling her of all the things they wanted to do in the neighbourhood and the most important one, of course, was to ride the General's horses.

They decided that tomorrow they would go to the stables and inspect them for themselves.

"As long as you be sure to leave me Dragonfly," Melva insisted, "I am quite prepared for you to have any horse you like."

Her cousins knew how fond she was of that horse and they promised her that if they stole all the others they would most certainly leave her with Dragonfly!

There was so much for them to talk about and so much news to hear.

It was only when Melva went upstairs to change for dinner that she realised that Mr. Stanford had not been with them.

She expected that he was in the stables.

At the same time even to think about him made her have a strange feeling.

It had moved in her breasts when he had kissed her.

She had never been kissed before and yet it was exactly what she thought a kiss would be like.

She had read so much about King Arthur and his Knights and they were invariably in her thoughts.

She had sometimes imagined herself being kissed by one of the Knights of the Round Table.

The kiss that Mr. Stanford had given her was even more marvellous than she thought it would be.

Then she remembered that he was married and she was quite certain from his point of view that it had just been a kiss of joy.

It had been given to her because they had escaped, so it had nothing personal about it.

But she knew that it was very personal and intimate to *her*.

She had to dress for dinner in a hurry with the maid helping her and so she did not have much time to think of anything else.

Then she walked slowly down the stairs.

Mr. Stanford was in the drawing room talking to her father.

When she saw him, she felt as if her heart turned a complete somersault and it was suddenly difficult for her to breathe.

However, it was impossible for her to speak to him because, as soon as she had appeared, her cousins and their friends, who had not gone home to change, surrounded her.

They were all asking questions or making plans of what they could do now that they were living next door to her.

"Of one thing you can be quite certain," her eldest cousin said, "we will have our own point-to-point and our own steeplechase."

"Before we do that," another cousin exclaimed, "I insist on us having horses of our own! I am not going to let Uncle Aubin sweep the board as he usually does with the best horseflesh for miles around."

"You will have to talk to Mr. Stanford about that," Melva said. "He is such an expert on horses and so clever with them. I am sure that he will find some outstanding ones without you having to go very far to look for them."

"The nearer the better," one cousin remarked.

She agreed with him.

A little late, because it took the butler some time to enlarge the table and lay it, they went into dinner.

Melva then found that once they were seated that Mr. Stanford, as an employee, was at the other end of the table and there was no chance of her talking to him during the meal.

The real trouble was that no one listened and, as they all had so much to say, it was very hard to be heard amongst all the noise.

However, Melva stole a glance at Mr. Stanford whenever she could.

She thought, although she knew that it was wrong to think so, that he was undoubtedly a Knight from the Round Table.

He was even more handsome than she imagined the Knights would be.

When they all moved into the drawing room after dinner, Mr. Stanford did not join them.

It was with difficulty that Melva did not go to find him and she was sure that he would be in the stables.

Finally Sir Wilfred said it was time for him to take his family and their friends to his castle.

"We will come over tomorrow morning," Melva's eldest cousin said, "and we will ride all round your estate. Then you must come over and see ours. I have a feeling, although don't tell Papa, that it's not as good as it should be."

"You will soon get it shipshape," Melva replied. "And, of course, we will help you in every way we can."

"All we want are horses," another cousin shouted out.

Then they were all saying over and over again,

"We want horses! We want horses!"

The General laughed at them.

He told them that if they did not behave themselves properly he would close his stable doors and then they would have to walk everywhere!

"You could not be so cruel, Uncle Aubin," they cried. "And, as you have the best horses in the whole neighbourhood, you cannot be so unkind as not to let us share them with you."

"I will take good care," the General replied, "that you buy your own as quickly as possible."

He looked round the room as he spoke and added,

"I suppose Stanford has retired to bed, but I will tell him in the morning to start supplying you with everything you will need."

The party piled themselves into their carriages that were waiting outside.

They said a noisy goodbye and were singing as they went down the drive.

Melva gave a deep sigh.

"It was fun to see them, Papa," she said, "but they are a little overwhelming."

"They will settle down," the General told her, "and it will be very delightful for you, my dearest, to have some young people to amuse you."

"I have been so happy with you here, Papa," Melva replied.

"I know that," the General answered. "At the same time you are young and you need young people around you. I know that I have been selfish and rather remiss in concentrating on my book. But now it is nearly finished we will have parties and perhaps a ball."

Melva knew that she was not as excited about the prospect as she would have been a week or so ago.

Once again she was thinking of the kiss she had received from Mr Stanford.

'It meant nothing to him at all,' she told herself, 'nothing! He is a married man and he was just delighted as anyone would be that we had escaped from those ghastly smugglers, who would have drowned us.'

"You are looking serious, my dearest," the General remarked unexpectedly. "What is worrying you?"

"I am not really worried, Papa. In fact I was just wondering if there were enough horses to go round."

It was a lie, but it was the first thing she could think of to say.

"I am sure that there are plenty and some over," the General said. "Now go to bed, dear child, and there will be no point in riding before breakfast or immediately after it. We will have to wait until the herd arrives."

He blew out the candles in the drawing room.

They walked up the stairs together and, when they reached Melva's room, she kissed her father and said,

"Goodnight, Papa. Altogether it has been a most exciting day, but I am feeling very tired now it is over."

"Of course you are, my dearest, so sleep well, as I know there is going to be a great deal to do tomorrow."

He walked down the passage to his own room and Melva went to hers, where the maid had left everything ready for her.

She walked over to the window and drew back the curtains.

There was a full moon overhead and the stars were shining brightly in the sky.

They turned the garden below into a misty silver paradise.

Melva found herself wishing that she could be there with Mr. Stanford.

Then she was shocked.

She had no right to be thinking so much about him all the time.

'He is married! He is married! He is married!' she said to herself over and over again.

Yet there was still that strange feeling in her heart and it had been there ever since he had kissed her.

'How could I be so foolish as to fall in love with a married man?' she then asked herself. 'He has gone to bed thinking of his wife and not me.'

She thought, in fact, that he considered her rather tiresome.

A silly young girl who had got them into trouble by taking him to see the smugglers' caves.

They had only been saved by her at first, then by his brilliant way of freeing themselves from the ropes that held them prisoner.

'I must forget him and think about those nice young men who are with my cousins,' Melva reflected.

Yet despite what she was attempting to do, she kept seeing Mr. Stanford's handsome face in front of her and he was always smiling at her.

She looked down into the moonlit garden.

She thought that she could see him there amongst the flowers and the trees.

He was wearing the shining armour of one of King Arthur's Knights.

How long she stood there she had no idea.

Finally she forced herself to undress and get into her bed.

It was impossible to sleep.

She kept feeling the touch of Mr. Stanford's lips on hers and the strange wonderful feeling that had risen in her breasts.

Although she tried to deny it, the feeling was still there and was growing stronger.

'I love him, I adore him,' she whispered to herself.

She knew that it was something she should not say.

Because she was so very tired she must have fallen asleep for a little while.

*

She awoke for no reason except that she thought that someone was calling her.

She had not pulled back the curtains before she had gone to sleep.

The stars were still twinkling in the sky, but fading a little.

She thought if she went to the window she would see the first flicker of dawn on the horizon.

'I shall see him soon,' she smiled to herself.

Then she wondered what she would do.

If she was honest, it would only make her love him more than she did already.

'I am going mad,' she thought. 'How can I at this moment, when everything is changing and all my cousins are here, think only of a married man who is not interested in me?'

She looked back and thought of the days they had ridden together and had talked about so many fascinating subjects.

Yet Mr. Stanford had been entirely impersonal.

He had said nothing and done nothing to make her think that he was the least interested in her.

Not as a woman, let alone one who attracted him.

'I expect his wife is very beautiful,' Melva said to herself.

She felt as if a dagger pierced her heart.

Because it was impossible to sleep, she climbed out of her bed and walked to the window.

She was quite right, the dawn was just beginning to creep up into the sky and very shortly the stars would be swept away.

Melva then thought that she must go to Dragonfly.

Because she was so lonely she had always treated Dragonfly as if he was her companion and friend.

Whenever she was unhappy, worried or perturbed about anything, she turned to him.

If her father was angry with her or something went wrong, she would run over to the stables and throw her arms round Dragonfly and tell him what was upsetting her.

She felt that he understood and it was almost as if he spoke to her.

He would say it was not of any importance and by tomorrow what was making her unhappy would have been forgotten.

'I must go to Dragonfly now,' she thought. 'Only he will understand. Perhaps in some magical way he will prevent me from loving a man who is married to someone else.'

She went to her wardrobe and put on the first dress that came to hand.

She was not going to ride Dragonfly, but just sit in his manger and talk to him.

She slipped on some flat shoes which would make no sound as she crept out of the house, not that there was anyone likely to hear her.

She did not bother to arrange her hair. She just left it hanging in golden waves over her shoulders.

When she was ready to go, she opened the door of her bedroom very quietly.

She knew that she need not be afraid that she might wake her father. He slept very heavily, sometimes snoring a little.

When she had been obliged to wake him, she had to shake his shoulders before he opened his eyes.

All the same, as she was doing something unusual, she went very quietly down the stairs.

She opened the door that led into the garden and as she did so there was an instant scent of flowers.

She realised that the moonlight was not as bright as it had been, but there was enough for her to see her way over the lawn.

She passed the fountain throwing its water up into the sky and it was catching the first gleam of light from the East.

Then she walked through the rhododendron bushes towards the stables.

She knew at this hour that all the stable boys would be asleep in their large cottage that her father had built especially for them.

It was a comfortable building and in many ways the grooms had to look after themselves.

Her father, however, was generous enough to have a woman from the village cook them one good meal a day and so they were never hungry. She also kept the place clean and tidy, although she thought it good for the boys to do most of the housework.

There had never been any trouble in the stables at night and so, unlike many horse owners, the General did not insist on one boy being kept on guard overnight.

As Melva now came through the rhododendrons, she looked towards the stable where Dragonfly was.

Then she stiffened and stood still.

To her great surprise there was a man just opening the outer door of the stables.

She peered at him trying to see a little more clearly who he was.

He was not one of the grooms nor was he Mr. Stanford.

Yet strangely there did seem something familiar about him.

Then, as she attempted to pierce the darkness, he opened half the stable door and moved inside.

As he closed it behind him, she could see his face.

She knew then, with a sense of horror, that it was the highwayman.

He then disappeared into the stables.

Melva looked across the end of the yard.

She could just see the gate that led into the paddock and there was a horse tethered there.

She knew then with a sense of horror that swept through her why he was here.

The highwayman was clearly about to steal one of her father's horses and it might easily be Dragonfly.

Moving swiftly, at the same time silently, she ran up the side of the stable yard.

She went straight to the cottage where Mr. Stanford was sleeping.

She ran so quickly that she was breathless by the time she reached the door.

As she put out her hand, she thought that perhaps he had locked it and if so it would be almost impossible to wake him without making a noise.

To her relief the door was unlocked.

She opened it.

As she knew the cottage so well, she did not have to guess where he would be.

She ran up the stairs propelled by an urgency that made her jump the last two steps.

She opened the door of the bedroom and rushed in.

The curtains were pulled back and, as the sky had lightened on her way to the stables, Melva could see that Mr. Stanford was asleep.

She rushed to the side of the bed saying urgently,

"Mr. Stanford, wake up!"

She thought that he could not have heard her.

So she put out her hand to shake his shoulder as she would have done to her father.

"Wake up! Wake up!" she cried.

The Earl, who had been fast asleep, then opened his eyes.

For a moment it was impossible for him to realise what was happening.

Then, as Melva called out to him "wake up!" again, he replied drowsily,

"Melva, I was dreaming of you."

"Wake up," Melva cried, "the highwayman is here. He is at this very moment stealing one of our horses and it might be Dragonfly."

The Earl was instantly awake.

"*The highwayman*!" he repeated.

"I have just seen him going into the stables," Melva said breathlessly. "Hurry! Please hurry or I am afraid he will take Dragonfly with him."

The Earl had learned to be quickly alert when he was in the Army.

"Go downstairs and wait for me," he said. "I will not be more than two minutes."

Because Melva was so frightened she did exactly as he asked of her.

She ran from the room and went down the stairs almost as quickly as she had come up them.

She peered through the open door.

For the moment there was no movement from the stables where Dragonfly was.

The door that the highwayman had closed was still shut.

The Earl put on his shirt and pulled on a pair of trousers with a swiftness he had learned as a soldier.

He was thinking that if Melva was right and the highwayman was there, he would need a weapon.

Then, with a large sense of relief, he remembered something.

When they had gone back to the chaise, Albert had handed him the reins and had given him the revolver.

He had told the boy to defend the horses if by chance anyone tried to steal them.

He himself was still considerably bemused by what had happened in the smugglers' cave.

Instead of putting the revolver back into its secret place in the chaise, he had slipped it into his pocket.

He had then forgotten all about it.

He took his coat down from where it was hanging in his wardrobe.

He found that the revolver was still there and he checked that it was loaded.

It could only have taken him two or three minutes before the Earl joined Melva at the bottom of the stairs.

She was peering through the window at the side of the door.

As he reached her, she said in a whisper,

"He has not come out yet. His horse is still by the gate into the paddock."

The Earl glanced in that direction and he saw the horse tied to the gate.

Then he looked at the door where the highwayman had entered the stables.

The Earl did not have to wonder if Melva was right in saying that he was still inside.

If he had come out alone, he would have ridden away on his own horse.

"Should we go and – see what he is doing?" Melva questioned.

She was obviously very frightened and her voice was almost incoherent.

"No wait!" he answered. "Are you quite certain that you saw him go through that particular door?"

"You can see he has left the top of it open," Melva replied.

"Yes, of course," the Earl agreed.

"Perhaps he is seeing which of the horses he likes the best. I am sure it will be Dragonfly."

She remembered as she spoke how she had been woken by the feeling that someone was calling her.

Because her blood was Cornish, she had often in her life been somewhat clairvoyant and had known things about people before she was told them.

She had been aware before her mother died that there was no hope of saving her.

She thought now that it might have been her mother who told her that Dragonfly was in danger.

Or perhaps the mythical Knight, who she identified as Mr. Stanford, had done so.

She had often pretended when she was out riding that a Knight was with her.

She was quite certain now that it was her Knight or the one who looked after Mr. Stanford, who had enabled them by sheer intelligence to escape from the smugglers.

'Please God, please let the Knights help us now,' she prayed fervently.

Because she was so frightened, without meaning to, she slipped her hand into the Earl's.

It was his left hand. He was holding the revolver in his right.

Because he realised how afraid Melva was for her horse, he said very quietly,

"Don't worry. I promise we will save Dragonfly whatever else happens."

"How can all these things happen to us?" Melva murmured almost beneath her breath.

"We have won so far," he replied. "You cannot be faint-hearted now."

"No, of course not, but Dragonfly means so much to me, I just cannot lose him."

The Earl did not answer her and after a moment she whispered,

"Surely we should go and see what on earth the highwayman is doing."

"No!" the Earl said. "You must trust me. Wait, I know it's the right thing to do."

Melva's fingers tightened on his.

"I do trust you and you have been so wonderful already. But he has been in the stables now for quite a long time."

The Earl did not answer.

He only knew that what he was doing was right.

It would be a grave mistake to take a wrong step that might prove disastrous.

Then, as Melva felt that she must plead with him again, they saw a hand.

It was on top of the closed part of the stable door.

A moment later the door opened.

Then Melva drew in her breath and she felt the Earl stiffen.

Next the highwayman came out through the door bringing Dragonfly with him.

It was quite obvious now in the early half-light to see why he had been so long inside.

Dragonfly was bridled and saddled.

Melva gave a little gasp, but the Earl was still.

Then, as the highwayman pulled Dragonfly into the stable yard, he saw the mounting block just a yard or so from the door.

Dragonfly was a large horse and the highwayman was not a tall man.

So it must have struck him that the easiest way to mount Dragonfly was from the block.

He walked towards it.

Dragonfly was not as skittish as he usually was in the morning and he made no protest as they reached it.

The highwayman then climbed onto the block.

The Earl released Melva's hand.

With a swiftness that made him almost invisible, he ran until he was within an easy distance of the block.

The highwayman was so busy putting the reins into his left hand and he only became aware at the last moment that he was not alone in the stable yard.

He turned his head to look at what had only been a fleeting movement.

As he did so, the Earl brought down his revolver, fired it and shot him in his right leg.

The highwayman gave a loud screech of pain and fell backwards onto the mounting block.

Melva ran from the cottage towards Dragonfly.

Even before the Earl was at the side of the fallen highwayman, she had her arms round her horse's neck and was hugging him.

Dragonfly had reared a little at the sound of the shot, but, now Melva was with him, he nuzzled against her as if to show how glad he was that she was there.

She did not wait for the Earl to give her any orders.

She led Dragonfly back into his stall and gently took off his bridle and the saddle the highwayman had put on him.

Enfolding her arms round his neck she sighed,

"You are safe, my precious. You are now back with me and no one shall ever take you away from me."

As if Dragonfly understood what she was feeling, Melva thought that in his own special way he was trying to comfort her.

Outside the Earl glanced at the highwayman.

His wound was bleeding and he was groaning and whimpering with pain.

The Earl did not go near him, but went to the house where the stable boys were sleeping.

Albert, having heard the report of the revolver shot, was already awake and he came to the door to see what was happening.

"A highwayman tried to steal Miss Melva's horse," the Earl told him.

"A highwayman!" Albert repeated.

"One of you go off immediately to inform the Chief Constable and ask for the Police to come and collect him," the Earl said. "The rest of you had better carry him in here and lock him securely in one of the rooms."

He paused and then continued,

"With a wound in the leg he cannot get away and it will be a very long time, once he is in prison, before he can menace other people or steal their horses."

He saw the excitement in Albert's face as this was just the sort of adventure the stable boys would enjoy and because the Earl had no wish to spoil Albert's fun, he left him.

Albert rushed upstairs to carry the news to those who were still sleeping.

Without hurrying himself the Earl walked back.

The highwayman was now not only groaning but he was swearing at his wound. He had managed to sit up, but it would be quite impossible for him to run away.

The Earl felt that it was not his horse's fault he had such an unpleasant master.

So he then released the highwayman's horse from the gatepost.

He took off his bridle and saddle and left him free to eat the grass in the paddock and there was also water there if he wanted to drink.

The Earl then went back to the stables where Melva was with Dragonfly.

He thought how sensible she had been to fetch him instead of confronting the highwayman herself.

Once again, despite her fear for the horse she loved, she had behaved with great bravery and common sense.

The Earl knew only too well that any other woman of his acquaintance would have been clinging to him and she would be crying and noisily hysterical.

'It is extraordinary for a young girl to have so much self-control,' he reflected, 'and at the very same time to be so beautiful.'

As he thought of Melva, he remembered what he had felt at dinner.

He had seen her being complimented and flirted with by the friends of her cousins.

She had not been embarrassed or shy as another girl of her age would have been – she had merely laughed at them.

What was more she had given intelligent answers to any questions they had asked her.

It struck the Earl now what had struck him before he went to bed.

He was completely certain that Melva would play perfectly, if she had to, the part of a Duchess.

She would do it without either being intimidated by the position or making a nonsense of all the necessary formalities.

Then the Earl told himself that this was something he did not want to think about that night.

In fact the sooner he went to sleep the better, but it had been impossible for him to do so earlier.

He kept feeling the touch of her lips against his.

He felt the tremble of her body as she unfastened his gag in the smugglers' cavern.

As the whole party moved noisily into the drawing room, one of Melva's cousins had put his arm round her shoulders.

The Earl had told himself that it was impossible for him to stay as things were.

He was sure that by the time he returned home the Princess would either have found another suitor or gone back to Germany.

At any rate, even if he did not go home, he could not stay with the General.

He felt as if his whole body was throbbing with that strange feeling that had overwhelmed him when he kissed Melva.

'If this is real love,' he thought, 'I cannot think why more people don't run after it.'

Equally he was forced to admit the truth.

It was a feeling that was so perfect and so unspoilt it might have come down from Heaven itself.

'Damn it all!' he said to himself finally. 'On some excuse or another I will leave tomorrow.'

It was then that he had fallen asleep.

Next he had been woken by Melva, who he was dreaming about.

As the Earl opened the stable door now, he knew that she would be in Dragonfly's stall.

She had saved the one thing she loved and he knew just how much the horse meant to her.

He was not surprised when he reached the stall to see that Melva, having unsaddled Dragonfly, had her arms round his neck.

He stood for a moment gazing at her.

She was exquisitely lovely with her fair hair falling over her shoulders.

Although he did not speak, she was aware of his presence and looked round.

As he entered the stall, she released Dragonfly and rushed towards him.

"You have saved him! You have saved Dragonfly!" she cried. "How can I ever thank you?"

Her face was turned up to the Earl's and she looked unbelievably entrancing.

Her voice seemed to sweep away everything that he was thinking.

His arms went round her.

"You can thank me like this," he answered as he pulled her gently against him.

CHAPTER SEVEN

The Earl raised his head.

"How can you make me feel like this?" he asked.

Then he was kissing her again, kissing her wildly, possessively, passionately as if he was afraid of losing her.

She felt as if her whole body melted into his.

She was part of him and they were one person.

She felt as if he was carrying her up into the sky.

The stars were twinkling in their hearts and she had reached Heaven.

As the Earl's lips finally released hers once again, Melva sighed,

"I love you, I love you. I know it's wrong – but I cannot help myself."

There was a rapture in her voice that he had not heard before.

"I love you too," he said simply.

Melva hid her face against his shoulder.

"It is very wrong and wicked of us," she murmured. "But it's so wonderful, so utterly marvellous. I did not believe that love could be like this."

"It is not wrong and it is not wicked," the Earl said a little unsteadily. "I have loved you from the first moment I saw you, but I have fought against it in every way I can. But, my precious, you have defeated me."

His arms tightened around her.

Then he said,

"How soon will you marry me?"

Melva made a sound of astonishment and looked up at him.

"Marry – you," she faltered, "but you are – already married."

The Earl smiled.

"That, my darling Melva, was a lie. I have never been married and I was determined not to be married. But I know it will be impossible to live without you."

"Can it really be – true?" Melva asked.

"I swear to you it is the truth," he said.

She gave a deep sigh that seemed to come from the very depths of her heart.

"If I can marry you," she said, "it will be the most wonderful thing that could ever happen to me. I will look after you and I am sure if we work very hard we will have enough money to live on."

The Earl looked at her.

He had thought it impossible to ever find a woman who loved him for himself alone.

And not to be loved for his position, nor his title.

"I believe with your help, my lovely one," he said, "we can do anything. Even conquer the world if that is what you want."

Melva gave a laugh and moved closer to him.

"All I want," she murmured, "is to be with you. I thought last night that if you went away my whole world would be dark and empty."

"As it is," the Earl said, "it is going to be very full, sometimes very difficult, but we will be together."

"That is what I want," Melva said, "and please can we be married – very soon? Otherwise I feel that, with all my cousins here – they will stop us being together."

"We will be married tonight or tomorrow if it is at all possible," the Earl said.

He kissed her again.

It was a long possessive kiss that made her whole body quiver with the rapture of it.

When he set her free, Melva realised that the sun was now shining outside and streaming through the stable windows.

It was morning.

"What have you done about – the highwayman?" she asked.

It was an effort to remember him.

Mr. Stanford's rapt kisses and his love had swept everything else from her mind.

"I suppose" the Earl said reluctantly, "I ought to go and see if the Police have arrived. I have told Albert to send a groom for them."

"It will take some time," Melva said. "You don't – think he could have escaped while we were here?"

"That would be impossible, but I don't want you to worry about it. Go into the house, my darling, and when your father comes down to breakfast I will join you. We have so much to talk about and plan before all your noisy cousins arrive to empty the stables."

"They are not to take Dragonfly," Melva asserted.

"No, of course not," the Earl agreed. "Nor will I have them riding my white horses."

He put out his hand to pat Dragonfly and then he turned and walked to the door of the stall.

"Go into the house," he said. "I don't want you involved in all this unpleasantness."

Melva did not answer.

She just watched him with love in her eyes as he left the stables.

She could hardly believe that she was not dreaming.

It was incredible that the man she loved so much also loved her.

They could be married!

She wondered now why he had pretended to have a wife.

But all that mattered was that he did not have one and he wanted to marry her.

Nothing could be more perfect.

"I love you, I love you, I love you," she was saying over and over again.

But she then left Dragonfly and walked slowly back through the rhododendrons and into the garden.

She stood gazing at the fountain and thinking how much it had been a part of her dreams all through her life.

Now her dreams would be filled with the man she loved.

She knew that his name was Clive.

She thought, as she had thought before, that he was exactly like one of King Arthur's Knights. And 'Sir Clive Stanford' sounded like a Knight's name, strong, firm and intrepid.

For the rest of her life he would be there to kill the dragons in whatever shape or form they came to frighten her.

She looked up at the fountain and then at the bright cloudless sky above it.

"Thank you, God, thank you," she sighed. "How could you have been so kind as to send Clive to me? He is everything I have ever wanted or imagined I could find in a man."

Because she was so happy, there were tears in her eyes, tears of happiness that were very different to the tears she had shed last night.

She walked back into the house and, having washed her hands, she went into the dining room.

She had only been there for a short time when her father joined her.

"Good morning, my dearest," he began. "I do hope you slept well. We are obviously in for a busy day today trying to keep those young ruffians in order!"

He kissed her cheek.

Then he walked towards the sideboard where the breakfast dishes were waiting and added,

"I will not have them being rough with the horses or they will not be allowed to borrow them again."

"I feel sure they will be very careful, Papa."

The General turned to her.

"You are looking very lovely today!" he exclaimed. "I have not seen your hair like this for a long time."

Melva had forgotten that she had not arranged her hair when she had climbed out of bed to go to Dragonfly.

It seemed totally impossible when she had been so miserable then that she should be so happy now.

Because she was waiting for Clive to appear she did not answer her father, but helped herself absent-mindedly to a dish of eggs and bacon.

"Now what I want to discuss with Stanford," the General said, "is which of our horses should be kept back to be exercised tomorrow. Then we will have a better idea of how well some of these youngsters can ride."

Melva did not answer and the General went on,

"I am not worried about Wilfred's sons, they have always been as good as he is. But the friends, of course, are an unknown quantity and so are the girls."

As he finished speaking, the door opened and the Earl came in.

"Oh, there you are, Stanford!" the General called out. "I want to talk to you about – "

Before he could finish the sentence, to his surprise Melva rose from the table and ran to the Earl's side.

She slipped her arm through his and said,

"I have been waiting for you before I told Papa what has happened."

The Earl smiled at her.

"It is something I am very eager to tell him."

The General was looking at them perplexed.

"What has happened?" he asked. "What is wrong?"

"Nothing is wrong," the Earl replied. "Melva and I have fallen in love and with your permission we want to be married as soon as possible."

"Married!" the General exclaimed as though he had never heard of it. "Married, but you two hardly know each other."

The Earl laughed.

"As far as I am concerned," he said, "I have found the wife I have been seeking for a very long time. And before I say anything more I should inform you that I am not who I pretend to be."

"Not who you pretend to be," the General repeated in astonishment, "then who are you?"

"My real name is Clive Bourne," the Earl replied, "and my father is the Duke of Shelbourne."

For a moment the General was numbed into silence.

Then he exclaimed,

"Shelbourne, I was at school with him. How could you possibly be his son and if you are, what on earth are you doing here?"

"It is a long story," the Earl said. "But to tell you briefly, my father ordered me to marry someone I had no intention of marrying, so I ran away."

He paused as if he was thinking what he would say next and then he added,

"My father would have expected me to go North, so I came South and as you know reached Land's End."

"I have never heard such an extraordinary story," the General commented.

Melva moved from the Earl's side to her father's and put her hands round his neck.

"All that matters, Papa," she said, "is that Clive loves me and I love him. So we want to be married very quickly."

"You are so like your mother," the General said. "When you have made up your mind, there is nothing that anyone can do about it."

Melva kissed him.

Then the General went on,

"Of course I am glad that my only daughter will marry Shelbourne's son. And I have always admired your father and his loyal support in the House of Lords has been extremely helpful to the Army."

"I thought that would please you," the Earl said.

Melva was very quiet.

Now she moved back to stand beside the Earl.

"As you are so much grander than I ever imagined you could be," she said in a low voice, "are you quite certain that you want me as your wife?"

The Earl put his arms round her.

"I have never and this is the truth, wanted to marry anyone and in fact I ran away from home because the idea was so repulsive. As I have already told you, my lovely darling, I cannot live without you."

The General was a very shrewd judge of men and, watching them, he knew that what the Earl was saying was with a sincerity that came from his heart.

As the two of them stood gazing into each other's eyes, he said almost sharply,

"Now with regard to this wedding, I imagine from what you have said that you don't want a grand ceremony with all your relations present."

The Earl sat down at the table and drew Melva into the chair next to him.

"What I want," he said, "and I know Melva wants too, is to be married very quietly with you, General, as our only witness. Then I wish to go away on our honeymoon where we can be completely alone."

The General smiled.

"It is what I would have liked myself," he said. "So I do understand what you are feeling. You can be married here in the Private Chapel or at Saint Ethelred's Church in Penzance."

"You have a Chapel here!" the Earl quizzed him.

"Of course we have," the General replied. "What Tudor house was built without one? But it is very small and the last time the Chapel was used was when Melva was Christened in it."

"Then that would be a lovely place to be married," Melva enthused. "And as – Clive," she hesitated a little over the name, "has just said, you, Papa, can give me away and also be – the only witness."

"I quite understand that you don't want that noisy collection from The Castle," the General. "But you two will have to behave very discreetly in front of them."

Melva looked at the Earl.

"We will try," she whispered.

"Would it be possible," the Earl asked, "for us to be married tomorrow or the following day? It is going to take us a long time to travel to my home and I would like to set out on the journey as soon as Melva has my ring on her finger."

"You are thinking of driving?" the General asked.

The Earl nodded.

"I have a rather better idea. My brother, Wilfred, is borrowing all my horses so I would suggest that I borrow his yacht from him for you two."

"His yacht!" the Earl exclaimed.

"It is in the harbour at Penzance," the General said. "It is very large and very comfortable and I should imagine unless you are in a tremendous hurry to get home, that you will enjoy taking Melva to the Mediterranean. You could show her a little of Rome, Venice and then perhaps on to Athens."

Melva gave a cry of sheer delight.

"Would that be possible? Oh, please, please take me there. It is where I have always longed to go."

"I will take you anywhere in the world if it makes you happy," the Earl said. "And, of course, nothing could be better than if we had a fine yacht to carry us there in comfort."

"Leave that to me," the General said. "I will tell my brother that I want to borrow his yacht and swear him to secrecy as to why it is required."

He looked happily at his daughter and went on,

"You, Melva, must take your fiancé to see the Vicar who has known you ever since you were a child. He will be delighted, I know, to marry you tomorrow evening if that is what you wish. As he has often pointed out to me, the Chapel being so old is still licensed to marry without banns, which only a very few Chapels in the country can now boast."

Melva looked at the Earl as if for his approval.

He breathed quietly,

"Nothing would make me happier."

"Now eat your breakfast," the General said. "Then we will all get busy before those noisy young people take the roof off."

He started to eat the food he had in front of him as he spoke.

The Earl thought, admiringly, that no man could have behaved better under the circumstances or been more helpful.

"Thank you, General," he said. "Thank you very much indeed from the bottom of my heart. May I say, after having worked here for you, I am very delighted and proud to be your son-in-law?"

The General was touched and responded,

"I can only say, my dear boy, that I welcome you not only because you are your father's son but because I have truthfully become very fond of you since you have been looking after my horses."

Melva gave a little cry.

"Dragonfly! How will we get Dragonfly to Clive's home, wherever it is?"

"There will be plenty of room for him," the Earl said quickly, "at Shelbourne Towers and, of course, I will want my white horses to be home when we go there."

"You can leave that to me," the General said. "It will be quicker and much less exhausting if the horses went by sea. While you are on your honeymoon, I will arrange for them to travel by ship from Penzance to Bristol or the nearest Port to Shelbourne Towers."

"I think that Southampton will be the best," the Earl remarked.

"Then Southampton it shall be. Just leave them in my hands. I have arranged a great deal of shipping one way or another in my life."

The Earl knew he was referring to the troops he had taken overseas and the guns and other instruments of war that had to go with them.

"I can only say I am very grateful for your help," the Earl said.

The General pushed his plate aside.

"As I think it very unlikely that my brother will accompany his children when they arrive here," he said. "I am going to ride over and talk to him about his yacht. I hope, Clive, you will wait to see that those who want to ride have horses allocated to them they can handle and then you and Melva can visit the Vicar."

"I will do that, General, and I will be very careful as to which horses are ridden by those who are not as experienced as your nephews."

"That is what I want you to do," the General said.

He rose to his feet and then bent down and kissed his daughter on the cheek.

"I have worried a great deal, my dearest, although you were not aware of it," he said, "over who you should marry. All I can say is that I am very delighted with your choice and very proud indeed that, because you are just as lovely as your mother, you will undoubtedly be the most beautiful Duchess of Shelbourne ever in the history of that illustrious family."

Then, as there was nothing more he could say, he went from the dining room closing the door behind him.

Melva looked at the Earl.

"I am quite sure I am dreaming," she sighed. "I thought I was marrying a poor man and was so worried in case he minded me having a little more money than him. Can it be possible that I am really going to be a Duchess?"

"You are really going to be my wife and you are going, my darling, to have to work very very hard, but in a different way to what you expected."

Melva drew in her breath.

"Suppose," she asked almost in a whisper, "I fail you?"

The Earl put out his arm to pull her nearer to him.

"The reasons I am so thrilled to have the yacht," he said, "is because I am going to teach you, my precious one, about love. And then about everything that concerns me. I shall need your help, your guidance and, most of all, your inspiration."

Melva looked at him.

"That is a wonderful thing to say to me," she said, "and I will try in every way I can to be exactly what you want in a wife. I don't mind what other people say because all I want is your happiness."

As the Earl could find no words to answer her, he kissed her.

For a moment they stood locked together.

Then with an effort the Earl said,

"I must go to the stables and prepare for all those excitable young people."

"I am now going to go upstairs to find a wedding dress," Melva said. "There are several for me to choose from because the brides who have been married from this house have usually left their wedding gowns behind them."

She looked up at him before she added,

"I want to look as pretty as I possibly can for you on our wedding day."

"You look like an angel who has come down from Heaven, my darling. When I came here, I was determined to marry no one, but after I met you, you captured first my heart, then my mind and now my soul."

"Is that really true?" Melva asked.

"I swear to you it is the truth, but just as I have to teach you about love, my beautiful one, you will have to teach me what you feel in *your* heart."

Melva gave a cry of sheer happiness and put her arms round his neck.

"I love you, I adore you," she whispered in his ear.

Then it was impossible to speak.

It was five minutes later before the Earl managed to leave the dining room.

As he went into the hall, he saw that the postman had called.

As was usual he had put the letters for the house on a table just inside the door.

The Earl saw that there was one for himself and knew it was from Nanny.

As he then walked through the garden towards the stables, he opened it.

To his surprise it was quite short.

Nanny had written,

"Dearest Master Clive,

I'm scribbling this to catch the post.

His Grace has just come back from Windsor Castle where he went yesterday.

What I have to tell you is good news.

Her Majesty, I thinks, was tired of hearing that you was still too ill to come to The Castle, so Princess Gilberta has now become engaged to Prince Ivan of Norway, who was paying an unexpected visit to England.

I thinks they fell in love, but it pleased Her Majesty to believe that as you didn't turn up as expected she had found a good husband for the Princess.

His Grace, Wilkins tells me, is relieved that he's no longer involved and be wondering how he can find you.

Wilkins says he heard him say, 'if Clive's married, then at least there's a chance of my having an heir to the title'.

No time for more,

Love and God bless you,

Nanny."

The Earl read the letter again and laughed.

It was so like Wilkins to know everything that was going on.

At least his father could not complain that his wife was not good enough for him.

Everything that he had felt was so disastrous and so upsetting was now solved.

There would be no need for him to apologise to his father or anyone else for eloping with himself!

He thought of Melva and how beautiful she was and how wildly in love he was with her.

And then he looked up at the sky.

'How can I be so lucky?' he asked himself.

It was a prayer of thankfulness that he could not put into words.

*

In the house Melva had not gone upstairs as she had intended.

Instead she walked to the Chapel at the far end of the house.

It was indeed very small which was why Services were seldom held there.

The Elizabethan windows were still intact and the altar that was made of a single piece of marble had stood there all through the centuries.

It was Melva's mother who had added a beautiful altar cloth to it when she was first married.

Six golden candlesticks to stand on either side of the ancient gold cross were also her gift.

Melva knew when the gardeners brought in every white flower from the garden that it would be a perfect place for her to be married.

She knew that it would please Clive as well.

As she thought of him, she went down on her knees in front of the altar.

It was impossible, she thought, to put into words her thankfulness to God for all that had happened.

Clive had saved her from the highwayman and then from the terror of being captured by the smugglers.

Finally he had made sure that Dragonfly was safe and had defeated the highwayman a second time. He really was her Knight in shining armour.

"I love him, I love him," she cried aloud looking up at the sun streaming through the stained glass windows.

"Please God make him love me not just for now but for ever and ever and then help us to give some of this wonderful Heavenly happiness to others, but most of all to our children."

It was a prayer that came from the very depths of her heart.

There were tears in her eyes when she had finished whispering it.

Then, as she knelt in prayer, she felt as if a shaft of brilliant light came from the altar and enveloped her.

It was a light so vivid and so ethereal that she knew it was Divine.

She was being blessed by God himself.

"Thank you, thank you," she whispered again.

She knew that the love which had just enveloped her would join her and Clive together not just for this life but for all Eternity.